THE BOOK OF LETTERS
FORBIDDEN BOOKS, VOLUME VII

DAVID MICHAEL SLATER

LIBRARY TALES PUBLISHING

PRINTED IN THE UNITED STATES OF AMERICA

Published by:
Library Tales Publishing
511 6th Avenue #56
New York, NY 10011
www.LibraryTalesPublishing.com

ISBN-13: 978-0998333489
ISBN-10: 0998333484

For Heidi, a love letter

"I cannot think it unlikely that there is such a total book on some shelf in the universe."
— Jorge Luis Borges

PROLOGUE
VERY, VERY WRONG

r. Brody, Chief of Staff at Oregon Health & Sciences University, let loose a long, defeated sigh. His tie was askew, his shirt halfway untucked, his slacks a wrinkled mess. Reluctantly, he approached the patient's bed, but before he got the chance to perform any sort of examination, a series of vicious thunderclaps, loud as bombs, exploded outside, shaking the entire building. The doctor was forced to steady himself with the bedrail until the room settled. When it did, he observed with disappointment, though not surprise, that the patient exhibited no awareness whatsoever of having slipped a bit in his sheets.

With practiced hands, Brody moved the long-suffering little man back into a comfortable position, making sure both the feeding and breathing tubes were still in place. He conducted a quick check of vital signs, then turned slowly around to express his displeasure.

"But—!" cried the tedious nurse who'd dragged him out of his office, "I—his eyes! They were—!"

"Your attachment to Mr. Picarelli is admirable, Nurse Cates," Dr. Brody granted, managing to stay calm for the moment, "but we've been through this before. Many times. It makes you oversensitive to insignificant—"

"But—!"

"The man has been in a coma for over a year. You are going to have to accept that he's never coming out of it. The fact that his family has enough money to keep him here doesn't change the—"

"But—!"

"Surely, Nurse Cates," Brody snarled, his depleted store of generosity all but exhausted now, "you are aware that the sky seems to be *on fire*. I'm betting you've noticed the little thunder problem as well—

the one that seems to be making everyone lose their minds?"

"Yes, of—"

A clamor arose just then: patients marching down the hall, shouting unintelligible demands while whacking the walls with metal bedpans.

When they'd passed, Dr. Brody resumed his reproach. "And perhaps you've also observed that the hospital is in a state of complete and utter— *Never mind,*" he huffed, waving this all away, waving Nurse Cates away. "I need to get back to work." He headed for the door but stopped abruptly when his cell phone buzzed in his pocket. Brody took it out, put it to his ear, and snapped, *"What?"* Then he shouted, "No! I haven't heard from her! *Yes!* The woman who works twenty-four hours a day, seven days a week, has gone AWOL for the first time in her entire bloody life!" He listened a moment, then said in a much more subdued tone, "The President?" and a moment later, "You're kidding me—The *Pope?*"

Nurse Cates clutched a small cross hanging at her throat.

"Do those idiots in Rome understand she's against everything they stand for?" Brody ranted. "Do they know *she's not a climatologist?* Forget it," he said. "Tell them we'll find her." Then he hung up. But instead of leaving, he just stood where he was, sweating right through his shirt.

"Dr. Fludd—" Nurse Cates ventured. "She took in the Wax twins, didn't she? Perhaps they all went on a getting-to-know-you trip of some—? Dr. Brody, are you feeling quite all right? I can see you are under a great deal of stress."

"I'm fine, Nurse. I'm busy. I'm *unbelievably* busy."

"It's just that—I couldn't help—You mentioned the White House. And the Pope—"

"Just before Roberta—*Dr. Fludd*—came up with the cure for the plague," Brody explained, "she spouted some nonsense to the President, something about monsters from the Garden of Eden, and it apparently got beyond the Oval Office—quite beyond. The Vatican evidently thinks we're in the midst of some kind of religious *event.* Jesus," he marveled, "you're the first person I've told that to. *I'm* losing my mind. You're not to mention it to anyone.

The press has been on us like jackals."

Nurse Cates, paling, nodded while her boss produced a laugh signifying anything but amusement.

"I'm quite certain she was rather close to having a nervous breakdown," Brody said. "We all are. *Were*. But perhaps she realized taking in two teenagers is even more difficult than staving off a pandemic and went off and had it. Especially those two teenagers—disaster-magnets, the both of them."

"But why would the *Pope*—?"

"They must truly be desperate. I'm telling you, when the Vatican starts advising governments on how to handle an ozone layer meltdown, you know all hell has broken loose. It is 112 degrees after all." Again, the crazy laugh.

"Shouldn't people—I mean, the pubic—" Nurse Cates asked, "Shouldn't they know the Pope thinks—?"

"The public should know what we decide they should know, and when we decide they should know it. Can you imagine what would have happened if they knew we had no cure until the very last second? I shudder to think. Now, I need to get back to my office. So, unless you know something the police don't know—"

"You mean—Do they think—Dr. Fludd—?"

"*Isn't her motto, 'I'll stop working when I'm dead'?*"

"Dr. Fludd *is* dead," someone said, someone who wasn't Dr. Brody or Nurse Cates.

Both doctor and nurse stiffened at the voice. After quickly looking at one another, they turned back to the comatose patient in his bed.

Who was no longer comatose.

"Though not legitimately or perhaps permanently so."

Mr. Picarelli was sitting up, holding the breathing tube he'd pulled out of his throat. His voice, rough and ragged from lack of use, sounded haunted. He was sallow and frail, but most definitely awake.

"I'm wearing a diaper," he said, looking down into his sheets.

"It's a miracle!" Nurse Cates cried. "I—I told you!"

"*Good God,*" was Dr. Brody's reaction.

"Wrong," the little man replied, shaking his head

in slow, wide arcs. "Very, very *wrong*." His sunken eyes were darkly amused.

Joy drained from Nurse Cates' beaming face. She took a step back.

"Dr. Fludd—" said Brody, recovering his professional air. "Did you say something about Dr. Roberta Fludd? How is it that you—?"

"He sent me back," said Mr. Picarelli, grinning now. "Picked me, he did. Me! Picker! I'll be FAMOUS!"

"He's delirious," Brody decided. "Which is hardly unexpected given that he's been—"

"She's up there," Picker said, glancing upward momentarily. "With *Him*. In the fire."

Dr. Brody had been slowly moving toward his patient, but stopped cold at this. "The fire?"

Picker grinned and merely pointed at the ceiling.

Doctor and nurse looked up, then turned to the wall, both finding it necessary to confirm what they already knew: there were no windows in the room.

"How could you—?" Dr. Brody began, but then he said, "Of course! You must have heard us discussing Dr. Fludd, and you heard me say the sky was on—"

"The sky isn't on fire," Picker said.

"It's not?"

"Heaven is on fire."

Nurse Cates crossed herself, then began whispering a prayer.

Dr. Brody ignored her. He said nothing for a moment, but rather just scrutinized his patient.

"He'll be here soon," Picker said. "I'll need a TV crew."

"A TV crew?"

"Yes. I am to explain His terms to everyone at once."

"Terms? Whose terms?"

"His, silly," Picker said, once again pointing at the ceiling. "He who unleashes the Fire. *The Red Dragon.*"

CHAPTER ONE
Too Late

Daphna was in the Light—she was in Heaven.

And it was on fire.

The Sacred Books of Heaven's Library, the innumerable multitudes of Sacred Books that housed people's souls—they were on fire, too. Hurled from their infinite Shelves, the Books were scattered throughout the Light. They were heaped in awkward, broken piles as far as Daphna could see in every direction—and the piles were in flames. And the Letters that should be teeming in their countless combinations upon the pages of the Books, the A's and C's and G's and T's— the Sacred Letters of DNA that gave form to Life itself—they were burning off the Pages, and the sound Daphna heard as they turned to smoke and ash was a howling too painful to bear.

Daphna ran madly through the Light, screaming names. "Quinn!" she wailed. "Are you here? Quinn! *Quinn!*" But the boy she'd fallen for wasn't the only one who didn't belong there. She also needed to bring his poor parents back. She had to find Nora, too, for her brother. And Dr. Fludd, whose reward for taking them in was getting torn from the world.

"Dr. Fludd!" Daphna cried, tripping and falling into a pile of burning Books, then scrambling back to her feet to run wild again. *"Dr. Fludd! Quinn! Nora! Is anyone—?"*

Daphna stopped. She'd arrived at a shelf still standing, a single solitary shelf standing alone in the Light, a shelf with only one Book on it, a Book she knew—*her* Book.

And for a moment, Daphna forgot everything but her Book. All was quiet and there was no fire. There was nothing but Daphna Wax and her Book. She reached out and carefully took it off its shelf. She knew the pages were blank, awaiting the return of her soul.

With trembling hands, Daphna opened it. To her horror, flames leapt from its pages, flames in the form of a Dragon, and the Dragon opened its jaws and an inferno burst from its throat, and Daphna could not avoid it.

Then the Dragon was gone and Daphna stood at the shelf holding her Book. Its pages were no longer in flames, which was a great relief, but her skin was so hot—so unbelievably, unbearably hot. Daphna dropped her Book and fell upon it in the Light. She tried to cry out, to offer one final apology to everyone she had failed, but it was too late.

She was burning.

Dexter and Nora were under the Portland Art Museum, in the Mason's secret lair, and there were the Colors, those strange, tall, but otherwise harmless, suburban-looking folks searching for their Book, their Holy Grail. They'd turned rabid, showing vicious teeth, and they were running up and down the walls, snapping the necks and spines of any Mason they could grab, but just as quickly they were being snuffed out by the Mason's blades and vanishing in bursts of Light. Dex was there, just standing there, in the middle of all the bloody mayhem, screaming "Stop!" But no one listened or even seemed to notice him at all.

But then they did stop, because they were gone, all of them, Mason goons and Colors alike, and it was just him and Nora and the leader of the Masons in his red mask, and he was threatening to scrape their names from the pages of the Book of the Living. And Nora approached the awful man on his throne, and she pulled his mask right off his face, and they all saw it was her father, as she somehow knew, and they struggled with the multi-bladed dagger he held to the page.

And Dex sprinted to help, screaming "Stop!" again. "Stop! Please, stop!" But though his legs churned, he saw that he was not moving at all. He screamed and wailed and drove his feet forward in a desperate frenzy, but he simply could not move. And when he tried to scream again he found that he could not speak.

And now he saw why. It was too late. He was strapped into the hideous wooden bench with the metal contraption built onto it, and the contraption was fitted over his face and the clamp on it had hold of his tongue.

And so Dex could not even say he was sorry when Nora and her father, still struggling, scraped each other's names out of the Book of the Living and vanished from this world. The best he could manage was to think the word as the clamp was retracted with a sudden, violent jerk, ripping his tongue out by the roots.

Blood poured from Dex's mouth. It poured out in torrents, and it wouldn't stop pouring. A river of blood flowed out of him, and it filled the chamber under the museum.

Dexter was alone then—and he was drowning.

CHAPTER TWO
One More Piece of Information

"I'm sorry!" the twins both cried. Then, at the very same moment, they opened their eyes.

It took a moment to register that they'd let themselves fall asleep on Mr. G's living room floor, but they were bloodied and bruised and far too weary to worry about it. They were alone, so they simply got up and limped to the front window to look outside.

Tears rolled down their faces as they looked up at the flaming hole in the sky. The crowd outside, having finished setting the high school on fire, was standing on the baseball field doing the same.

The twins had seen so many awful, impossible things, but this was perhaps the worst. It was like seeing the fabric of reality burning itself up.

"*Nora,*" Dexter whispered.

Daphna choked, "*Quinn.*"

"I imagine you've figured it out."

Dex and Daphna spun round, tensed to fight or run, neither of which they were actually capable of doing. Fortunately, Mr. Guillermo looked equally out-of-sorts. His face was drained of color, and blood, dripped out of his hair, was streaked across his cheek

It was strange to see him without his glasses, Daphna thought. His face, without them, was somehow more noticeable, and more noticeably odd. His eyes were set too close together, and they were a funny kind of pale green. His skin, under stubble, seemed shiny. *Did the whole glasses routine mask that? Daphna wondered. Or is it just that nobody really ever looks closely at teachers?*

Mr. G was looking ruefully at the stolen painting of the Last Supper, which was still lying on the floor—a rendition he was supposed to have destroyed because it depicted Jesus holding up a golden book rather than, as in many versions, a certain famous cup.

"If you mean, did we figure out the Holy Grail is a book," Dex said, "then yes, we did." He didn't feel the least bit guilty for nearly braining Mr. G. The guy had almost broken his nose—not to mention tried to kill him. Actually, now that Dex considered the matter, he wanted to hit Mr. G again. The trophy he'd used was on the floor, too. Dexter found himself eyeing it.

"Take a deep breath," Daphna urged. "Through your nose and down all the way into your belly." She could see the hostility surfacing in her brother's speckled green eyes. She felt it as well. It was like the searing heat outside was drawing out her worst impulses, like perspiration. She took several long, deep breaths the way she'd advised.

For his part, Mr. G seemed uninterested in further violence. He joined the twins at the window to look at the vortex of flames spinning and spurting in the sky.

Maybe Quinn isn't still up there, Daphna hoped. His body was surely in that secret operating room in the clinic downtown, already recovering from—whatever went wrong with the Standstill operation. She was sure that last shot was to blame, the shot he'd been given after being killed, then revived, but declared still in Heaven—the shot of clear fluid that smelled like tarragon. She had to find out how he was as soon as possible. *Sooner,* because who knew how long it was going to be before everyone succumbed to this—this *Evil Urge*—spreading, it seemed, like another plague. Daphna could see it working right there on the street where the rioters—kids and adults, alike—were shoving each other around.

She had to get up there, not in a dream, but for real, right up through that flaming hole if need be, to make sure the souls of the people she loved were not destroyed. She'd even save Wren, that crazy Popular who'd wanted her dead. She'd even save Nora's horrid father, who'd tried to erase their names! She'd find Mr. Brown and submit to the Standstill operation herself so she could go and make things right for everyone, once and for all. It should have been performed on her, anyway!

Breathe, she told herself.

A thunderclap shook the world just then, shooting mighty jets of orange and crimson flames out of the swirling hole—terrifying, elongated tongues that threatened to reach right down to the ground. At the sight of them, everyone on the street finally saw fit to take cover.

"I have to find it myself," Mr. G muttered when the flames were sucked back into the hole and the house stopped shaking. "I have to. I *will.*"

"Maybe we can help each other," Dex said, looking up from the painting. He'd been staring at Holy Grail—the Holy *Book*—held up by Jesus to his robed Disciples at their long table. The book was not well defined. It was just a blurry gold rectangle, though maybe it looked clearer to people whose eyes could handle light bouncing off the things they were trying to see or read properly—people without Scotopic Sensitivity Syndrome.

"We know you purposely taught at all our schools," Daphna said, looking challengingly into Mr. G's peculiar eyes. "So you could spy on us our entire lives. We know you've been watching and waiting 'till one of us was going to die so you could tell us to come back from Heaven with the Holy Grail, or Holy Book, because you think it's hidden there."

Mr. G shook his head, looking profoundly defeated. "That's all true of course," he admitted, "but I don't even have the slightest idea how or why you could possibly do that. You see," he lamented bitterly, "I was never deemed worthy of all the facts—of *any* of the facts."

"Then you just work for Mr. Brown?" Daphna guessed. "You're not one of the—the Colors? I've been calling them that because of all their names. I guess your name isn't a color."

"Oh, I am one of them," Mr. G replied, "but at the same time, no, I am not. I'm not a fully-fledged member—never earned my wings, as they say. What I know—*everything* I know," he added darkly, "I've learned through my own research. They gave me a job—watching you, documenting your every move—a job that conveniently kept me away from them, isolated and alone."

"Well, they wasted your time," Dex said, rather unkindly, "'cause the Book probably isn't even in Heaven. All the angels are searching for it up there, and I'm pretty sure they've been searching for it since—forever."

"Dexter," Daphna said, "you don't need to be cruel. There are billions of books up there. Trillions. It could be there." She felt downright awful for Mr. G now. His whole interest in world religions was evidently nothing more than an attempt to discover what larger story he was but a bit player in. *But then,* she thought, *isn't that everyone's lot in life?* Everyone's but theirs, it seemed. A bit part was all she wanted! "We have extremely rare extra ribs," Daphna explained.

"Intrathoracic ribs," Dex put in.

"Right. We're two of thirty-six people alive—"

"Who are *supposed* to be alive," Dex corrected, back to staring at the book in the painting. A *book,* he thought. *Of course the Holy Grail is a book.* So unless he was somehow perfected by Heaven's light, he'd need Daphna to read it. He'd need *her* to save Nora.

"Who are *supposed* to be alive," Daphna conceded, "at any given time. The ribs can produce stem cells that generate life all by themselves.

Dex didn't care who saved Nora. He couldn't think about anything else but getting her back. The guilt he felt for drawing that innocent girl into the ghastly mess that was his so-called life was hollowing him out. She wasn't even really dead—Dex was sure of that. She was only gone—to Heaven, surely—having had her name erased from the Book of the Living. If she'd been lost in the fire up there, he would—If the souls of his dead mothers, his real mother and first adoptive mom, Eve herself, had been lost forever—and Dr. Fludd was there too, also erased. If that all happened—If *any* of that happened, he'd find the Grail, and he'd read it whether his eyes cooperated or not, and he'd use it to put the whole damn world out of its misery once and for all. He'd put a big fat 'The End' on the planet's last page.

The thought filled him with something disturbingly close to pleasure.

"Go on," Mr. G was saying to Daphna when Dex tuned back in.

"The 36, we're called Lamed Vavniks in Hebrew, or The Righteous Ones—though we're pretty sure now that being righteous isn't really part of the job. Anyway, my rib can create spontaneous life while I'm alive, because I'm a girl. But both of ours can if we're dead and buried."

"God's insurance policy," Mr. G whispered, sounding awed.

"Yes! That's exactly—"

"The 36," Mr. G continued, his eyes somewhere else. "If mankind ever wipes itself out, one of you would bring it back. Life would once again rise from the ashes, the dust, the clay—Incredible! The others—?"

"Killed," Daphna said. "And their ribs permanently destroyed."

"Then you are the last!" Mr. G cried. "Do you know what peril the world would be in should something happen to—?"

"We *know*," the twins moaned.

"There's more," Daphna said, trying not to let the fact that mankind's survival might depend on their own, or their extra ribs' survival, anyway. "Both of us, for a short while, after we're dead—" she continued, "the ribs can bring us back to life somehow, if our bodies haven't been destroyed. But only for a short time, a month or so at most, I think."

"Maybe that's what *he* did," Dex said. He was pointing at the painting, at Jesus. "We know his mother had the rib, which explains his unusual birth. So maybe he had it, too, because that would explain his unusual death."

"Wow, Dex," Daphna said, shocked and amazed by this rather casual revelation. "That's—that's—"

"One more piece of information to get us killed."

CHAPTER THREE
A List of Ingredients

"*My God,*" Mr. G gasped, "you two are not only living proof that the Virgin Birth has an alternate explanation—but that the Resurrection does too!"

Daphna nodded, unsure how to feel about this latest news—other than profoundly uneasy.

"That certainly explains why I was told you might be killed by Church assassins."

"And you would have let them kill us," Dex snapped, "if we didn't make you think we'd already found the Grail. You would have let anyone kill us!"

"Breathe, Dex."

"You breathe!"

"I assure you it would have pained me to see you perish," said Mr. G. "You two are the closest things to a son and daughter—to family—I have ever had."

Dex nearly laughed out loud at this.

Daphna could not dwell on the absurdity of the statement because the Secret Keeper of the Church and his assassins had, until just now, mercifully slipped her mind. The power behind the Pope had come to Portland all the way from the Vatican, personally, to deal with them. He could be anywhere out there in all the chaos. The weight of it all began to settle on Daphna. She closed her eyes and drew in a deep breath, trying to let the urge to scream pass. But that breathing was hard to do sometimes.

Mr. G had squatted down by the painting and seemed to be staring intently at Jesus' face. "Interesting," he muttered to himself. "This is all *very* interesting."

"Good," said Dex, walking back to the window. "Now tell us who those Color people were."

"We know they weren't human," Daphna said, opening her eyes again. "Or normal human, anyway—that's for sure."

"*What?*" Mr. G was suddenly back on his feet

and back from wherever he'd gone in his thoughts. He looked desperately between the twins. "What did you say?"

"The Masons—" Dex started to say.

"The Freemasons?"

"Yes. They were searching for another book called The Book of the Living. They got it from us and had it under the Art Museum when the Church assassins came in. The Mason's leader, who turned out to be my friend Nora's father, scraped most of them out of The Book of the Living. But then the Colors came in and started killing the Masons with their bare hands. They were snapping their bones like balsa wood. They were running up and down the walls, jumping over people's heads."

Mr. G was white as a sheet. "But what did you mean who 'were' the Colors?" he demanded. His freaky eyes were nearly popping out of his head.

"Dex," Daphna said, "he doesn't know what happened. How could he?" She turned to Mr. G and said, "They—they killed all the Masons down there, but they were killed in the process."

"Killed?" Mr. G looked faint. "Not Mr. Brown—?"

"No, not Mr. Brown. He wasn't there." She didn't add that he was too busy having his doctor temporarily kill Quinn. "He's the last one left."

Mr. G looked mightily relieved. "But you must only think the others were killed," he said. "Because that's just not possible. It must have only appeared—"

"The Masons—" Daphna explained, "they had daggers dipped in some kind of liquid that smelled like tarragon."

"Qeres?"

"Yes!" Daphna cried. "Someone called out something like that!"

"It's my fault!" Mr. G suddenly wailed, utterly beside himself. "It's my fault! It's all my fault!" He staggered over to his desk, spluttering, and fell into the chair there, completely undone. "For the love of God, Qeres! No!" He actually tore a gash into his shirt. Then he slumped over onto the desktop.

"What is Keres?" Daphna asked, too desperate to see her teacher's breakdown as anything more than one more obstacle to finding out what she and her brother needed to know. "I think that's the same thing they injected Quinn with," she told Dex. "I smelled tarragon in the operating room. I think it's what made the procedure go wrong! What is it, Mr. G? *What is it?*" Daphna was losing her cool, but she worked to settle herself down. Breathing. Breathing.

As calmly as she could, Daphna tried again. "Mr. G, what is Keres?"

Mr. G suddenly sat up and looked at her with wide, wet eyes. "They injected your friend with it?" he asked, strangely calm now. "Why in the world would they do that?"

"I—I don't know," Daphna told him. "They said they were trying to kill him for a moment, to send him to Purgatory. Mr. Brown thought the Holy Grail might be there, since it's the one place no one in Heaven or on Earth has looked, other than some sort of well that it sounded like they'd get killed if they got near. But anyway, Quinn went to Heaven when the doctor killed him, not Purgatory. He woke up—sort of woke up, I guess—screaming about the fire. They said he was still there and gave him the shot that smelled like tarragon, and he went into a coma."

"Purgatory?" Mr. G said. "Are you sure Mr. Brown used the word *'Purgatory'*?"

"Yes, Purgatory. He was lying wasn't he? There is no such place. He lied to us the whole time. He told us they were looking for something called the Book of Creation, a book that supposedly lets you create anything by combining letters and numbers."

Mr. G seemed not to have heard this. He was staring at Daphna, though his eyes were once again clearly seeing something else. He was thinking hard. Now he stood up, approached the painting, and squatted down next to it again.

"Just tell us what the hell Keres is already!" Dex was just about to lose it.

"Qeres—with a 'Q,'" Mr. Brown muttered. "It's the only substance in the world known to kill—" But he didn't finish the sentence.

"Mr. G!" Daphna urged.

"A perfume created in Ancient Egypt—" he added, but nothing more.

"Mr. Brown said the Masons go back to the Pyramids!" Daphna cried, having turned to her brother. She was certain they were about to learn something crucial. This was a feeling by now she knew better than to trust, but it nonetheless put her on high alert.

"It's the only substance in the world known to kill *what*?" Dex demanded.

Mr. G stood up and looked at the twins clearly for a moment, then said, "Why don't I just show you?" Then he turned, walked to his desk, and swept everything on it to the floor: computer, printer, notebooks, papers, books. Then he sat down, produced a key tucked under the chair somewhere, opened the locked drawer, and begin taking out a number of vials and containers.

"A few months ago," he said, "Mr. Brown gave me a list of ingredients to gather, ingredients that are very rare and difficult to obtain." He picked up a glass tube filled with a blue liquid, then used an eye-dropper to transfer drops from it into a tall beaker.

"Are you going to make Qeres?" Daphna asked. "Do you know how?"

But Mr. G seemed to have stopped listening again. He was adding a green liquid to the beaker, squinting as he did so at the measuring marks on the side of the glass.

Dex moved to pick up the trophy, but Daphna put a hand on his arm and gave him a look that made him want to hit *her* with it. He took in one of those stupid breaths, then forced himself to take another. They didn't have time for this. Nora needed him *now*.

"Of course he didn't tell me what it was for," Mr. G said, apparently responding to his own thoughts while pinching some kind of powder into the mix. "Brown never told me *anything*. But I discovered that one of the ingredients is a rare plant once used in Ancient Egypt in a pigment for painting."

"*And*?" Dex said.

"And so I took the list to a friend, hoping for a clue about what the recipe was for."

"*And*?"

"And this friend works at the Portland Art Museum."

"*Great*," Dex sighed. "Perfect."

"He was a Mason," Daphna realized. "Mr. G accidentally gave the recipe to the Masons, who knew what it was for. That's why he thinks it's all his fault the Colors got killed."

"Why didn't he tell me what it was?" Mr. G asked—begged really—looking up from adding something like ground plant material to the beaker. His eyes were swollen and red. "I eventually discovered what it was myself, but it was too late! Why would he want to make Qeres? I don't even know what the Grail really is! Though I think I've discovered that, too."

"Will you tell us what it is?" Daphna asked, sensing that remaining calm—and perhaps following Mr. G's lead in this conversation—was the wisest course of action. The concoction he was making was becoming opaque.

"We told you a lot," Dex said when no reply seemed forthcoming. He was done sucking in air like some kind of sick prank caller and fed up with the mad-scientist routine. The next time he had to ask about that Keres, or Qeres with a 'Q,' or whatever it was called, he was going to do so with the trophy upside Mr. G's head.

Mr. G was pouring a red liquid into the beaker now. He didn't look up, but he did finally speak. "The Grail," he said, "the *Holy Book*—it is the Book of Letters—a book that can put the almighty powers of Heaven in the hands of its reader."

"How?" the twins both asked. They held their breaths, hoping he'd continue this time.

Mr. G raised his head and looked between Dexter and Daphna with his weird, weird eyes. "Unless I am very much mistaken," he finally answered, "by revealing the secret Name of God."

CHAPTER FOUR
The Book of Letters

"The secret name of God?"

Mr. G got a funny look on his face at the sound of the twins' voices overlapping again.

"To be more precise," he said while adding drops of a sludgy black fluid to the beaker, "it contains instructions for *pronouncing* the secret Name of God, the unutterable Name—the 'Tetragrammaton' it's called—which is just a fancy word that means, 'the four letters.'"

"Are they the same as DNA?" Daphna asked. "A, G, T, and C, right?"

"That's a truly fascinating thought worth investigation," said Mr. G, who paused in his work for a moment to look up at Daphna. "The four letters of the Secret Name are Y-H-V-H, or Yud, Hey, Vav, Hey in—"

"Hebrew."

"Do you two often speak as one?"

"No."

Mr. G let this go. "What is not known are the vowels needed to pronounce the letters. In ancient times, the vocalization was known, though only to the High Priest—the Kohen Gadol—of the Temple of Jerusalem, who uttered it, once a year on Yom Kippur, and only in the Holy of Holies, which was the most sacred chamber in the Temple. Some believe this was done to ensure God's protection of the Jewish people for another year. But after the First and Second Temples were destroyed, the knowledge, like the High Priests themselves, became a thing of the past."

"So there's no one who knows how to say it?" Dex asked.

"Not unless there's a Kohen Gadol rattling around somewhere." Mr. G sounded amused by the very idea.

"But the Book of Letters shows the vowels?" Daphna asked. "So the pronunciation could be relearned if someone had it?"

"It is believed so," Mr. G told her.

"How does Jesus fit into this picture?" Dex asked, looking back at the painting once again. "How did he get the book?"

"Actually," said Mr. G, pinching a white powder into his beaker now, "some believe he was, himself, a Kohen Gadol. It is said that after the destruction of the Temple, the book was hidden away, kept safe in preparation for the coming of the messiah—the savior—who would surely read the Name when he arrived to save the world. Remember, Jesus was Jewish, and some Jews believed him to be the messiah. It's possible, quite likely even, that among those who believed, were those in possession of the book, and if that was the case they would surely have given it to him."

"Yom Kippur," Dex said, only half hearing all of this after the holiday was mentioned. "That's next week, isn't it?"

Mr. G nodded. "Ten days from today."

The twins shared a desperate look. Suddenly they could hear the ticking clock hanging over their heads—a ticking time bomb.

"That other book we mentioned," Dex said, "the Book of the Living. Have you heard of it?"

"Of course," Mr. G replied, swirling his mixture. It was completely clear now. "According to legend, one's name must be sealed in it each Yom Kippur to ensure the chance to live another year of life. I certainly hope it is no longer in the hands of the Masons."

"Unfortunately, it is," Dex said. "Though I sort of stabbed it."

"You sort of stabbed it?"

"To keep the Masons from using it," Daphna explained. "Dex stabbed it with a scary dagger that has six blades."

"I see. Pulling the blades out will risk removing names, names one can't see."

"Do you know," Dex asked, pleased to hear Daphna approve of his spur-of-the-moment plan, "if someone's name was removed and they, sort of, disappeared, or went to Heaven but without officially dying—Would they come back if their names were put back in the book before the ten days were up?"

"*Can* names be put back in?" Daphna added. She held her breath, hoping for the right answer. She could see her brother doing the same.

"The power to remove one another from this world, " Mr. G replied, "has always been in mankind's hands. But *adding* a life? That is well beyond—"

"Could we do it with The Book of Letters?" Dex asked. "With the secret Name of God?"

"Yes. Or perhaps with some other powerful instrument of creation. After all, Sacred Books were actually written at some time, with some tool."

"Any chance you happen to have one?" Daphna asked. "Or know where one is?"

"I'm afraid not."

"Then we're going to find the Grail," Dex declared.

The twins sighed. Ten days. They had ten days to find The Book of Letters and use it to bring back the people they loved.

"Breathe, Dex."

"You breathe!"

"I have a question," Daphna said, turning back to Mr. G, who was holding up his beaker and inspecting it closely now. "You said saying the secret Name in the sacred chamber got the Jews protected for another year, but you also said the Temple was destroyed. Twice I think you said, and it was forever, right?"

"Yes," Mr. G acknowledged, sniffing his potion again. "Some believe that the last Kohen Gadol pronounced the Name incorrectly, and thus the Jews were denied God's protection. And the rest was history—which, for the most part, as I'm sure you know—hasn't been a particularly well protected one for the Jewish people."

"*Wow,*" Daphna said.

"The tradition holds that anyone who utters the Name improperly—some say anyone who is not a Kohen Gadol who even *tries* to utter it—who even tries to *read it*—would be struck dead, struck instantaneously dead. Dead, it is believed, in both body and soul."

"*Dead in soul?*" the twins gasped.

"So you wouldn't even go to Heaven?" Dex asked, reeling.

Mr. G looked up again, his odd eyes now solemn and penetrating. "That is correct," he confirmed.

"But—where would you go?" the twins both begged.

"To the Realm of Dead Souls," Mr. G said. "Though it is impossible to know anything of it, for there is no return—though the Colors, as you call them, know of it now."

This alarmed the twins.

"But why would they go there?" Daphna asked.

Mr. G continued to work silently.

Daphna summoned her patience. "That story about reading the Name wrong," she said. "It sounds like a good way to encourage people to mind their own business. I'm guessing not everyone believes all that struck-instantaneously-dead-in-both-body-and-soul stuff."

Mr. G nodded as he dropped tiny pellets into his beaker, which fizzed before dissolving. "Some believe that uttering the True Name grants anyone," he said, "from the Kohen Gadol to the lowliest slave, the powers of God Himself, which is why only the High Priests were trusted with it, and only once a year."

"Wow," the twins both said. Both of their expressions had transformed entirely at these words. *This is it,* they thought. *Once and for all, this is it.*

"Others," Mr. G added, "think merely holding the Book of Letters transfers significant power—the power to perform miracles. Minor perhaps, but very real."

Dexter felt buoyed again by a rising tide of hopefulness. His emotions were rollercoastering the way they used to—so long ago now. He was starting to get the feeling that nothing that had happened to him had really, truly, changed him, that his experiences had all been nothing more than cruel, tantalizing illusions. He used to be able to perform miracles with just a Word. *One more!* He just needed one more! But maybe he wouldn't even have to try to read the Name! Maybe just holding the book would be enough. He'd never even hope for anything else again. He just wanted Nora back. He could see her pale eyes and wild frizzles of white-blond hair. Their lips had been inches apart, but he hadn't kissed her.

"Still others," Mr. G went on, "believe the High Priests never actually could read the Name—that they only made a formal attempt each year after spending just about every minute of the rest of their lives practicing it in meditation. It is suggested that if they ever could have pronounced it properly, they would have had the power to summon God Himself and, what's more, force him to do their bidding."

"*That* makes sense," Dex said, "since God took a hike so people could have free will."

"Wait—so we might be bringing God back?" Daphna asked. She looked at her brother and he knew what it meant: *That's what Dad was trying to do.*

"Well," Dex said, "he's perfectly welcome to go away and hide again—after we say His Name and make Him send everyone home."

"This whole name thing reminds me a bit of Rumpelstiltskin," Daphna said, trying to ignore the uneasy feeling seeping into her. "The girl defeats him by discovering his name."

Mr. G nodded and flashed a glimpse of the pleasure he so often displayed in class when Daphna made astute observations. "There are many, many stories in religion and folklore involving the power of true names." He tasted a tiny drop of his potion with the tip of his little finger. "They no doubt originate with the story of the One True Name," he added, "which is no doubt the source of all stories about magic words, or Words of Power as they're sometimes called. Did you know the word 'grammar' derives from a word that meant 'magic'?"

"Yes," Daphna said. She and Dex shared one more look, this one to say they both understood that if the world were a book, there was only one story in it, a story with infinite variations, perhaps, but one story nevertheless.

And they were both somehow certain The End, one way or another, was coming once and for all.

Daphna sniffed the air. "Tarragon!" she cried. "Mr. G—why are you making Qeres? Please! What does it kill? Tell us what's going on!"

Mr. G. smiled ruefully and poured one last vial into his potion, which turned it chocolate brown. Daphna immediately sniffed the air again. "It's gone," she said. "The tarragon smell—it's gone. What does that mean?"

Mr. G raised his beaker as if to give a toast and held it out to the twins for a second. "I will miss you two," he said. "Terribly, I think. You are remarkable, resourceful, truly admirable young people." He swirled and sniffed his mixture one more time and added, "You are the best of what this world has to offer."

"You don't want to go up there," Dex warned, not particularly alarmed that Mr. G was evidently preparing to kill himself. What business was it of his? "Trust us," he added, anyway. "We took an evil man into the Light. He opened a Book—a locked Book with a key in the cover—and the fire came out. That's what's happening. Heaven is on fire. It's burning down, and the heat is leaking out through the sky."

"Quinn—my friend," Daphna added, trying not to panic, "he said there was a dragon!"

"That is unfortunate," Mr. G replied. "But it's been clearly established that my help is neither effective, nor desired. The least I can do is join those I've destroyed, wherever they may be."

Mr. G put the beaker to his lips.

"At least tell us who the Colors were!" Dex shouted.

"Stop, Mr. G!" Daphna pled, leaping toward her teacher.

But it was too late. Mr. G swallowed the potion in one gulp.

"Tell him justice has been served," he said, setting the beaker down. "Tell him he's finally rid of me—and forever."

"Tell who?"

"My father."

"Your father?" Daphna asked. "Who is your father?"

Mr. G got up and staggered to the front window. He had to lean on the glass to support himself.

"Tell him I know where it is," he whispered, and tell him it's too bad he came too late." He tapped feebly on the glass.

"Dex!" Daphna cried, pointing outside. "Look!"

There, standing in the street and looking directly at them, was Mr. Brown. He was not dressed, however, in his casual slacks and sweater. Instead, he was garbed in flowing white robes. Around his waist was a golden belt supporting a long sword sheathed in a golden scabbard. And from his back stretched forth a pair of spectacular ivory wings.

CHAPTER FIVE
Whatever Had Been Freed

"Angels!" Daphna cried. "Qeres is the only thing in the world that can kill *angels!*"

Seeing the winged creatures drifting among the infinite Books in Heaven was one thing. Seeing one standing on the sidewalk on Vermont Street was quite another.

"But how—?" Dex started to ask, gaping at the resplendent wings. He looked around the room at all the pictures of butterflies. It was obvious now that the focus of every shot was the wings. "There's no way Mr. G has those wings. They're way too big to hide. But, how did Mr. Brown—?"

"Fledged," Daphna said. "He said he wasn't a 'full-fledged member.' That means feathers. I didn't think he meant that lit—"

"Tell him I'm sorry I never earned my wings," Mr. G croaked, turning to the twins. But then his face turned blue and he collapsed.

Despite the distance, it was clear that Mr. Brown could see what was happening. When Mr. G fell, the angel's face went instantly dark, as if a curtain had dropped behind his shining eyes. And then he was suddenly flying at the house. Before the twins could look at the door, it was down, smashed down, and Mr. Brown was there, already holding his son in his arms.

And he was weeping.

"Why?" he demanded. "Why, my son? My son!"

Something was happening to Mr. G's body. It was going blurry, soft around the edges.

He was turning to Light.

"Qeres?" Mr. Brown asked. His youthful hair, which was swept across his forehead, was wet with sweat. His cheeks were wet with tears.

"Yes," Daphna said, but then, "and no. Or sort of. He put something else into it—at the end. I could tell because the tarragon smell went away, just like in the operating room with Quinn!"

Mr. Brown appeared to want to ask a question, but before he got the chance there was an explosion outside, a shattering sonic boom louder than anything the twins had heard since the supposed thunder began, and it literally blew the sky open. Flames erupted from the vortex, and they poured down like molten lava from the heavens.

From Heaven.

Mr. Brown held nothing now but a soft Light in his arms, and then even that was gone.

Without a word, he leapt back outside and launched himself up into the sundered sky.

The twins ran outside behind him, pleading for him to wait. There was so much Mr. G had not told them. They both gasped at the hot air invading their lungs. It had to be 115 degrees. Wilson High School burning down across the street made it even worse.

The vortex was now disgorging a colossal pillar of fire, but Mr. Brown flew straight toward it, pumping his incredible wings with incredible speed.

"He's trying to get back in!" Dex shouted over the nearly deafening sound of falling fire. "The Colors—the angels! They must have given up searching Heaven for the Book of Letters and left to look for it on Earth! And I bet they couldn't get back in! This is his chance!"

"Dex," Daphna said, taking her brother's arm. "I think he's trying to get there before his son."

Either way, he was going back into Heaven, and this filled both twins with wild fear and hope. Side-by-side, they watched the angel race toward the pillar of fire spewing from the hole between the worlds.

But it wasn't a pillar—not quite. The leading edge was ragged with the flickering edges of its flames. And in that flickering there appeared to be some sort of figure. It looked almost like a—

"Dragon!"

The head of a dragon was taking shape, a monumental head encircled with blazing horns. But then, no—there were more heads: seven heads, all with massive, yawning maws.

A seven-headed fire dragon was coming down from the sky.

The twins both felt faint with déjà vu—they'd seen something like this before, something on a scale dwarfed by this horror. But Mr. Brown did not veer away. He drew his sword, long and gleaming in the sky like a band of stars, and pointed it at the dragon's heart.

Suddenly, black flames spewed from the thing's seven throats. The streams of fire enveloped Mr. Brown, blotting him out completely.

There was a brief burst of Light in the flaming darkness.

And just like that, the last of the angels on Earth was lost.

The twins stood there, gobsmacked.

The dragon was gone, but the pillar of fire continued streaming down. They heard screaming, though no one was around that they could see. It was coming from—everywhere, it seemed, including their own mouths now. And then the pillar of fire touched down, *punched* down, somewhere not terribly far away.

The ground rocked, knocking them off their feet.

From their backs, they watched a prodigious spray of dirt and debris burst into the air like a geyser over Southwest Portland. They covered their heads as clumps of dirt, grass, branches, and leaves rained down all over the street. It pelted them for a solid fifteen seconds, and then—all was quiet.

"The sky," Daphna said, brushing dirt off her face. "Dex, look at the sky."

Dex was already looking at the sky. The flaming hole was gone, as were the cracks and the waves of heat that had been pouring out of them. There were clouds floating up there now, just clouds, regular white clouds floating on the breeze. It was already noticeably less hot.

But neither twin took this as a good sign. They knew why the world above was peaceful again: whatever had been freed from that locked Book in Heaven was now on Earth.

CHAPTER SIX
One More Person

On her back, surrounded by steaming clumps of turf, Daphna took a long and deep breath down through her throat and into her belly. She held it there, then slowly let it out. She tried to concentrate on trapping the breath for just a split second before letting it out, sensing that if she could cycle the breaths without stopping for more than that instant, they would work even better. But it was rather challenging when what she really wanted to do was scream and rip out her hair.

She could hear her brother next to her struggling to calm himself, too.

It was hard to keep it together. So hard.

"He was *half* angel," Dexter suddenly said. He was sitting up, swiping grass chunks out of his hair.

"What?"

"Mr. Guillermo. He didn't explode into light like all the Colors when they got stabbed. He just sort of faded away. He must have had a human mother, and that's why he wasn't really one of them. That's why Brown didn't really like him, I guess. I think he added some kind of regular poison to the Qeres, and that killed his human part. The Qeres only kills the angel part."

Daphna sat up and shook her head. She was so drained and so sad. She just wanted it all to end.

Neither twin spoke for a few moments. They just sat there on the still-baking sidewalk.

"At least that thing isn't up there burning books anymore," Dex finally said. But then he realized something. "It—it couldn't have—You don't think—?" Now that they'd learned no one knew what happened to dead souls, he couldn't face the thought of Nora's soul having been snuffed out.

"No way," Daphna said, closing her eyes on the world again. "Like I said—there had to be trillions of books up there. It couldn't have burned them all, especially if it was spending its time trying to break out. Nora is safe with it being down here now, Dex. Our mothers and Dr. Fludd are safe. And Wren. And Quinn—"

"Who's probably not even up there."

Daphna opened her eyes and looked at her brother, but she did not respond to this. While it was true that Quinn might not be there—*God*, she hoped he was out of his coma—the icy tone of Dexter's remark infuriated her. But rather than lash out, she forced herself to close her eyes again and breathe. Then, instead of exploding into a trillion pieces, she opened her eyes and stood up. "Let's make a plan," she said, brushing dirt and grass blades off her arms and legs.

Dex got up with equal resolve. "We have one," he said, brushing himself off, too. "Find the Holy Grail—even though no one can find it on Heaven or Earth, not even angels—pronounce the secret Name, drag God out of His hidey hole, then make Him put everyone's names back into the Book of the Living, wherever it is. We can tell him get it back from the Masons and put it somewhere safe—permanently safe. And then He can admit abandoning the world to its own devices was a curse not a gift because mankind would be far better off without free will. Then we'll make Him fix everything, once and for all—including bringing back the other thirty-four Lamed Vavniks so we don't have to walk on eggshells for the rest of our lives."

"Right," Daphna confirmed, encouraged despite the sure impossibility of what had to be done. "That's exactly what we're going to do, though I don't think making God admit anything needs to be high on our list of priorities."

"We're going to make him to apologize, Daphna."

Daphna let this go, disturbed by the even colder tone in Dexter's voice.

The twins stood there for a few moments, just looking at each other, breathing.

Dex looked away. The layer of green park debris on top of all the houses made them look a bit like Hobbit holes, he thought. Quaint almost. The cogs in his mind were finally, if slowly, starting to turn again. "Wait," he suddenly said, turning to Daphna, "Mr. G said he knew where the book was!"

"Dex, look out!"

Dex spun around to find two teenagers, a boy and a girl, charging at him and his sister. Not gang members. Not jocks or jerks or Pops. Just a boy and a girl dressed in first-day outfits. They halted in front of the twins with their fists up, twitching and insensible with the need to hurt them.

"Breathe," Daphna counseled them. "Take a really deep breath down into your—"

The girl swung at her. Daphna ducked, though the punch grazed the top of her head. When she came back up, she laid the girl out with a fist to the cheek. Dex watched this, stunned for a moment, but when the boy came at him, one punch put his attacker on the ground as well.

The twins regarded each other for a moment, both appalled and impressed with what they'd become.

This was who they were now.

"Great," Dex sighed, looking up the street.

Daphna turned to see what he was looking at. More kids were cresting the hill up beyond the high school.

"Come on!" Daphna cried. "Before they notice us! In the house! We'll use the tunnels!"

The twins sprinted back toward Mr. G's front porch, but Daphna stopped dead after no more than three steps. Dex nearly knocked her down running behind her. "What are you—!" he started to complain, but then he saw.

Branwen was in the house. She was standing at the front window staring at Daphna with wide, unblinking eyes. Her famous raven tresses were twisted in a filthy, tangled mess. Her skirt and blouse were soiled, her right eye black and swollen from Daphna's first knockout punch.

She was holding a carving knife with the point set on the window, aimed at Daphna.

"Damn it!" Daphna fumed.

One more person who wanted her dead.

Dex had forgotten about Branwen, that deranged Pop who'd been driven even more insane by the need to revenge the loss of her best friends, Wren and Teal, which she blamed them for, especially Daphna for some reason. Even now, he couldn't help noticing that despite looking like a homicidal maniac who'd been dragged through a sewer, she was beautiful.

"Dr. Fludd's!" Daphna cried, turning away. She saw that the crowd on the hill had caught sight of them. The kids were already running. It was as if they somehow sensed the twins weren't like them, not yet anyway.

"Bikes!" Dex cried.

Dozens of bikes still lay strewn across the school's playing fields, so the twins ran for them. Wilson was an inferno now. The air around it was almost too scorching to bear, but they fought their way through it to the edge of the grass and managed to drag two girls' bikes to the sidewalk by the pink and white tassels on their handlebars.

But it was too late, anyway—the mob was on them.

CHAPTER SEVEN
Right Then

"Stop!" someone yelled just before the twins were seized. "A rich guy lives here!"

And just like that, the dozens of hands ready to tear Dex and Daphna limb from limb retracted, and the mob rushed across the street to a house a few doors away from Mr. G's.

"Let's go!" Dex cried, scrambling onto his bike. Daphna didn't need to be told twice. She jumped on hers, and the twins took off. Daphna shot a quick look at Mr. G's house. Branwen was gone.

Fortunately, there was no one on the street below. The elementary school across the field was also abandoned. Windows were smashed, but it wasn't on fire. Dex, ahead of his sister, flew around the corner just past it.

People. Lots of people.

A crowd was on the street there, brawling. Just regular folks: paunchy fathers in khakis, moms in business suits. One lady was wailing on an abandoned coffee cart with a bent putter. The twins kept to the sidewalk, and they almost avoided the melee, but someone threw something into the spokes of Dex's back wheel—an umbrella. Dexter flew right over the handlebars and hit the pavement hard, tearing skin off his hands—which at least helped keep the skin on his already bruised and bloodied face.

Someone was on him now.

Daphna screamed when her brother fell. She skidded to a halt, but before she jumped off her bike to—she didn't know what she was going to do—two big men ripped the man on Dexter right off him. Now they were pounding the guy in the face.

It was madness.

"Go!" Daphna cried.

This time it was Dex who didn't need to be told twice. The umbrella had dislodged itself, so he scrambled back onto his bike and jammed the pedals round. Daphna was right behind him, shaking with relief at another bullet dodged.

Once they reached the main road, where there was only a snarl of wrecked cars, the twins turned left and flew down to Dosch, then pedaled furiously up the hill to the upper part of their horseshoe-shaped road. There was rioting at both the church and synagogue across the way: sounds of shouting and shattering glass. But their street was clear.

Soaked in sweat and practically melting from the still nearly unendurable heat, Dex and Daphna forced themselves to pedal up the slight rise to Dr. Fludd's house. No one was there, so Daphna dropped her bike, ran to the garage, and punched in the code on the security panel. Dex was right behind her. The moment the door began to rise they dropped to the ground, rolled under it, then ran to hit the button inside that lowered it again.

Daphna headed directly into the kitchen, but Dex stayed behind a moment, considering Dr. Fludd's gigantic yellow Hummer. He glanced around and spotted a pegboard with several sets of keys hanging on it. Upon closer inspection, he found a set on a Hummer keychain. He took it over to the behemoth, climbed inside, and loosely inserted the ignition key. Finally, he headed to the kitchen.

Dex washed his hands, then dove into the giant sub-zero fridge, where Daphna was already standing, stuffing her face with cheese and grapes. He came out with packages of cold cuts, which he also devoured simply standing there. Daphna snatched some from him, then gulped down orange juice straight out of the bottle, now completely over her recent loss of appetite. Dex drank nearly an entire quart of milk.

When she was done pigging out, Daphna went around lowering shades and turning lights off, all the while ignoring the sirens multiplying outside. It was just starting to get dark. She pretended not to hear the helicopters. But then an amplified voice boomed from one of them: "Mandatory curfew by order of the President of the United States. All citizens are ordered into their homes and to remain there until further notice. Anyone outside of their homes will be subject to *immediate arrest."*

Daphna nodded, approvingly. At least they'd be safe for the night. Maybe. Until the cops lost it. But at least those in public service, those in any of the helping—the *selfless* professions—would be the last to lose control of themselves. They better be. She hurried around making sure all the windows and doors were locked. Once that was done, she called out, "Showering!" and headed upstairs.

Finally full, Dex took a look around at all the high-end gadgets in the fancy kitchen and decided it was not possible that it was just that morning he'd done the very same thing before heading out for their first day of high school. It was inconceivable that since then, he'd found and lost a girl he seemed destined for, discovered and destroyed a book with pages that kept people alive or wiped them off the face of the Earth, and the world had just about gone up in flames. But, then, what else did he expect? A typical day in the life of Dexter Wax. He headed up for a shower, too. Another perk of their new spoiled lives: they had their own bathrooms.

An hour later, the twins met in the hall outside their bedrooms on the second floor. Daphna had taken the time to tame the mess her bob had become, but Dex, whose hair was always a thicket of random spikes, just let it do whatever it wanted. But both had on fresh jeans and Paradise Books T-shirts, a mutual protest against the loss of the store they'd never opened—one more disappointment in their lives.

They smiled momentarily at their twinship.

But Daphna was distraught.

"That's what I was trying to say," Dex said. He'd also had time to follow the line of thought he'd begun before that mob nearly maimed them. "Mr. G said he knew where the Book of Letters is, but he killed himself—his body and his soul—rather than tell us, or his own father. He really must have hated him."

"But you saw Mr. Brown," Daphna said. "He was completely devastated. I don't need to see any more than what I saw to know he loved his son."

Dex was unable not to think of their own father—the father who happened to be the first man ever to live; the father who loved God more than man, more than *them*—the father who tried to make sure they fell to their deaths in the caves at Eden's edge so he could bring God back from the exile He imposed on Himself. And here Dex was trying to do the very same thing.

Like father, like son.

"Well, if he loved Mr. G," Dex said, taking in a deep breath, "he had a funny way of showing it. And because of that, we don't have the slightest idea where to begin."

"But Mr. G figured it out while talking with us," Daphna pointed out. "Something we said helped him. What did we say? Maybe we should go research those Cone Gable people."

"Kohen Gadol."

"Right. Or dead souls." Chilled again by those two words, Daphna headed into Dr. Fludd's office without waiting for Dexter's opinion on the matter. "I bet there won't be anything that hasn't been studied a thousand times," she muttered over her shoulder when she saw that he was following her.

"We told him we knew why he was watching us," Dex recalled.

Behind a large mahogany desk was a treadmill facing a flat screen TV on the paneled wall. The rest of the room was mostly shelves with medical books.

"Then," Dex remembered, "when he said he didn't know how we could return from the dead, we—you—told him about our ribs."

"Right," Daphna said. She'd settled into the desk chair and was searching for the computer's power button. "He said it was all 'very interesting.' Darn this fancy shmancy thing. Oh, here it is."

"Then I said maybe Jesus had the rib and that's how he came back from the dead."

Daphna stopped watching the screen come to life and looked at her brother. "Dexter," she said, "that's it! Right after that he started making the Qeres."

"Not exactly," Dex said, sitting down on the edge of the desk. "He stared at the painting of Jesus for a while, at the Holy Grail, or the Book of Letters, I guess. You told him about Quinn getting that shot so he could go to Purgatory, but—"

"He didn't say anything when I told him I thought

they lied about that," Daphna recalled. "But I got the distinct impression he knew there was no such thing."

"Of course he knew they were lying," Dex said. "Qeres doesn't send you to Purgatory. It kills angels."

Daphna wasn't shocked that she'd been lied to. How could she be? Not even being lied to by an angel surprised her. But she was panicking again for Quinn—what they'd tried to do to him. *"But why would they inject Quinn with it?"* she cried. "He obviously wasn't an angel!"

"What exactly did they do to him again?"

"They cooled his blood and gave him a shot that stopped all his vital functions." Daphna shook at the memory of Quinn with his eyes taped shut on that metal table. "Potassium something. Then they woke him up I guess, but only sort of, and he was raving about seeing fires in Heaven. The doctor said he was actually still there, and that's when they gave him the Qeres."

"Right then?"

"Yes, right then. Why?"

"Because right then he *was* an angel," Dex realized. It was all so obvious now.

"Oh, my gosh, Dex! That's true!"

"Since Mr. Brown was convinced the Grail wasn't in Heaven or on Earth, then he must have thought it had to be the Realm of Dead Souls. So he had to temporarily kill Quinn's body—to turn him into an angel. That way he could get a crack at temporarily killing his soul."

CHAPTER EIGHT
That Breakthrough Look

I'm sorry, Quinn!" Daphna cried as color poured over her cheeks. "I'm so sorry!" She'd allowed him to risk not only the life of his body, but the life of his very soul. She was going to fall apart, right here, right now, not knowing where or how he was. Nauseous, Daphna couldn't even sit upright, so she let herself slide off the chair and onto the plush office carpet where she lay on her back to breathe.

While Daphna despaired, Dex kept thinking out loud. "Apparently," he said, "your doctor didn't get it right, though, or what they were trying to do is just not possible. So, Mr. G knew right away they were lying, that they were really trying to kill a soul. He didn't know about our ribs, though. And—" Dex tried to replay the whole scene at Mr. G's in his head, which was hard because he'd been so aggravated the whole time. When he was trying not to pick up the trophy, he was staring at the painting. "*Wait*," he said, jumping back to his feet from the edge of the desk, "he spent a lot of time staring at the painting again after all of that. At Jesus—"

"You said that," Daphna groaned. But when she saw her brother's face, she got up. He had that breakthrough look. "What?" she asked. "You got it! *What?*"

Dex did get it, because he'd been thinking of their father earlier. "Mr. G thinks Jesus stole the book," he said. "Or he thinks that's what Mr. Brown thinks, anyway."

"*He thinks Jesus stole the book?*"

"Jesus loved man, right?"

"Well, yeah, I guess so."

"Maybe more than anyone, like, ever."

"Okay."

"So maybe the Book of Letters never was in the hands of the High Priests. Maybe they only went through with the ritual every year to make people feel protected, which worked I guess, until it didn't anymore. Meanwhile the book was exactly where it was supposed to be."

"In Heaven."

"Right. Jesus had the rib, so he had the ability to come back for a time. Maybe he *stole* the book because it had the power to summon God. Maybe he wanted to—to—"

The twins finished the realization together: "Bring God to man."

Daphna jumped back into the chair and attacked the keyboard, bringing up a search engine. After typing a bit, she waited, then read, "'In Christianity the Resurrection of Jesus refers to the return to bodily life of Jesus three days after his death by crucifixion. It is a key element of Christian faith and theology. The Resurrection of Jesus is not to be confused with the Ascension of Jesus into Heaven forty days after the resurrection.' Forty days, Dexter!" Daphna cried. "That's pretty much a month—exactly how long our ribs are supposed to let us come back!"

"So he was in Heaven for three days, stole the Book of Letters, then came back for forty. What did he do during that time?"

Daphna scrolled a bit and read. "Looks like he just appeared to a bunch of people to encourage them to follow him."

"What about the miracles? Walking on water and all that?"

"He probably did them during this time!" Daphna cried. "Just by possessing the book! Those details could easily have been moved into his earlier life, to make what happened later more believable! That's common in mythmaking! I bet he was taking the book around to show people, to convince them to—"

"To get them ready for the—what do they call it?"

"The Kingdom of God."

"Right."

"Dex," Daphna said, looking at him with that fire in her eyes that only fruitful research could kindle, "we're right. I know we're right. This is why the angels are searching the shelves in Heaven—they don't know he stole it!"

"Then what happened? He obviously didn't summon God."

"Dex, don't you see? He read the Name. But he—"

"Wasn't really a High Priest."

"Or he read it wrong. Which meant his soul was lost. And if he took the Book of Letters with him—"

"Then naturally no one searching Heaven or Earth would ever find it."

"Mr. G figured all this out," Daphna said, "and then sent himself to the Realm of Dead Souls—to punish himself in the worst possible way."

"To punish his dad, too, maybe. Unless he thought he could somehow bring it back to earn his wings."

"But how could he do that with no one to revive him?" Daphna asked. "I don't think he had hopes of doing anything useful, Dex. And what if the book isn't even there? What if it's still on Earth, still hidden? Why do we think Jesus could take it with him to the Realm, anyway? The rest of the Colors seemed positive it's here, in this well thing. Maybe they've thought all this through before us."

"How are we supposed know?"

"We've got to get back to the clinic and ask that doctor, if he even really is a doctor, and find out what he knows about it all."

"I'm sure Quinn's fine," Dex said. "There's a curfew, remember?"

"But Quinn was *there!*" Daphna pressed. *"In* Heaven. He might have seen Nora. He didn't have time to tell us everything he saw before—"

"What we need to do is find the Book of Letters," Dex insisted, though he now did want to go to that clinic. "If we find it," he said, "it won't matter what condition your boyfriend is in. We'll fix it. Let's do some research."

Simmering again, Daphna breathed, trying to tamp down her rage. Dexter couldn't even be bothered to pretend her feelings for Quinn mattered to him. But she recognized that there was no way they could venture out tonight safely. "Fine," she said, "we'll keep digging. But not now. I have a splitting headache. I'm going to snap once and for all if I don't get some rest."

Dex nodded. That was a fair description of how

he felt as well. They'd figured out enough for the time being. Unless they were completely wrong, which was probably the case.

"I'll get a few hours of sleep," Daphna said, "then I'll come back and see what I can find. You can just sleep 'till morning."

"Because I'm useless?"

Daphna didn't even dignify that remark with a response. She just walked out of the room.

CHAPTER NINE
The Room

Daphna collapsed onto her luxurious, king-sized bed. Her back, sides, and neck were aching beyond belief from nearly being kicked to death by Branwen in the tunnel underneath Mr. G's house. Her entire body was grateful for the softness and support. She was sure the tears were going to start flowing, but they didn't, and that was just as well.

Laying there with nothing else to do, Daphna looked around the gorgeous room she'd moved into just last night: her very own sleek and shining white desk with computer and printer, the soft carpet, the closet as big as her old bedroom, the empty bookshelves just waiting to be filled. They should already be filled with her photo albums, but they, like just about everything else in her life, had been lost. All her memories. She supposed she could fill them with the thousands of pictures—her and Dexter's every single day—lying in heaps all over Mr. G's secret room, but they'd all been taken without their permission and so felt like a violations. She'd never look at them again.

Daphna forced her thoughts back to her infuriating brother. She knew it wasn't all him. His anger was hers as well, though he seemed less interested in controlling it than she was. But she knew *some* of it *was* him, and that 'some' was the part that didn't give a damn about Quinn. But then, why should he? He'd only just met the boy—like she had. But he'd come to care about Nora just as quickly, and at least Daphna could respect that. He'd said he was good with Quinn being in love with her. But she had to admit she thought it was pretty outrageous herself at first.

She and Dex, as was their destiny, were alone, alone together perhaps, but with dreams and desires that had, in the course of a single day, diverged. A fault line had somehow opened up between them, something that seemed impossible after they'd become as close as they had. Daphna was terrified by the certainty that this had nothing to do with the Evil Urge festering outside. If that's all it was, they could try to fight it off.

No, this was something else, something inside them. How were they supposed to fight themselves off? So far they'd both managed not to fall into the gulf stretching between them, and that gave Daphna some hope. But no matter how often she and Dex shared the same thoughts, or spoke the same words, she knew the truth: they were growing apart. Was this something twins suffered through worse than other siblings when they grew up?

Quinn.

How could she be laying on hundred dollar sheets while he was on some quack's cold metal table, maybe in a coma or dead with his eternal soul at risk? She would never, ever forgive herself if he died. What if that crazy doctor tried to kill his soul again?

Curfew or not, she should be making her way back downtown right now.

But Dex would never agree to it. Not in a million years.

Should she go by herself? Separate *again*? After swearing to herself she'd never do that again, no matter what? But maybe it was wiser to be apart so that they and their ribs could not be destroyed together. It would be much more difficult for the Secret Keeper's men in black to hunt them separately.

She wished she could just give him their stupid ribs.

Wait a minute! Daphna thought. Why couldn't they? Why hadn't she thought of that before? It was the perfect solution! They could have surgery to remove the extra ribs, and the Secret Keeper could bury them in his little secret cemetery and never have to worry about Dexter and Daphna Wax ever again. The fate of mankind would be safe forever, along with the rest of his precious little secrets because who would believe anything a couple of perpetually troublemaking teenagers said?

Would they die without the ribs? But no, two more Lamed Vavniks would be born with them a month later. They'd be passing the buck to two innocent people who never asked for the responsibility of protecting the future of mankind.

But she'd never asked for it, either!

"To hell with it," Daphna said right out loud.

She picked her cell phone up from the bedside table, but after dialing, got the same message she'd heard before staggering into the shower: the networks were down and wouldn't be accessible for at least twenty-four hours. What did she think she was going to do anyway, ask information for the number of the secret, no-doubt highly illegal operating room in a health clinic somewhere in downtown Portland?

Daphna put the phone down, then picked up the picture she'd set against her lamp while changing clothes, the now crumpled picture of her at six years old, wearing all white at the Central Library, the picture that proved Quinn was in love with her—and had been in love with her since he'd seen her in his dad's bookshop wearing that same outfit. The thought that he'd always remembered exactly what she'd been wearing the day he'd first laid eyes on her filled her with—there was only one word for it—joy. Unbridled joy. Quinn risked his life to prove to her there were good, caring people in the world whose every thought and deed weren't aimed at ruining her life.

She should go without Dex.

Daphna got up and tiptoed to the window. Shouldn't one of them at least keep watch? If the house's silent alarm went off, would anybody even come? She doubted it. What were they going to do if they were attacked? She pulled back the blind a bit and peeked outside. It was dark out there and the shadows promised only harm. There were people, at least one, a dark figure, sprinting down the street. A door slammed somewhere in the other direction.

Daphna's heart was racing. With a sweaty hand, she pressed the blind back against the window and hurried back to bed. If Dex really thought Quinn could help him with Nora, they'd be downtown right now. She was sure of it.

Did she care about Nora? For Dexter's sake, yes, she did. She really did. But he only cared so much about her because she needed him like nobody ever had—because he could save her. Because he could be her hero. He probably thought he was in love with her, but he was only in love with the role she was letting him play.

Of course Nora had saved their lives by stopping her fanatical father from erasing them from the Book of the Living. She didn't deserve to have been erased with him—that was for sure.

A terrible thought wracked Daphna: What if she had to choose between saving Quinn and saving Nora?

Between saving Quinn and saving Dexter?

Oh, God, Daphna thought, throwing an arm over her eyes. Of course it would be Dexter, but either way, she could never live with herself.

Life was complicated and demanding enough, and now this.

All the pandemonium since she'd left Quinn had allowed Daphna to push thoughts of him away—or to ignore them, anyway—but now her feelings broke over her.

She *was* in love with Quinn—but no, she wouldn't think about him.

Branwen came to mind. Poor, pathetic, impossibly gorgeous Branwen, standing in Mr. G's front window with murder in her eyes. Her life had been ruined. With Teal dead from the plague and Wren erased from the Book of the Living, it was no wonder the girl was out of her mind. Being a Pop was her life, but there seemed to be no more meaning to the word. To think it was only two years ago that Bran and Wren and Teal were the three queens of middle school, back in an ancient history when having the right outfits, hairstyles, and vacation homes were what mattered most in the world. When just being the most beautiful girl anyone had ever seen gave you all the godlike powers you could ever desire. Daphna couldn't help thinking it: *They got what they deserved.*

But at the same time, Daphna wished she could just go back. Back to being the shallow little bookworm Pop-wannabe she was until the day her father came home from Turkey with a ruined book, the day before she turned thirteen.

Books.

How were they supposed to find the Book of Letters when neither humans nor angels searching this world and the next for centuries had managed? How were they supposed to find it if it was in the Realm of Dead Souls—or didn't even exist anymore?

And the Dragon, Daphna thought. *What is it?* She'd have to look up books as traps or prisons. She'd have to look up the death of souls, for that matter. And angels—*communicating with angels!* That would be first.

But she needed some sleep. Just a little sleep.

Quinn, Daphna thought, trying not to hyperventilate. *Quinn! You're going to be okay.* She laid her arms by her sides and started what she was now calling Feather Breathing, and it immediately began to settle her nervous system. She was getting better at it. A few times she felt as if the breath she took in reached her inner core, brushed it like a feather, then departed. That was what she was going for, but it was hard to repeat. She decided to count the breaths, and doing so helped distract her from her thoughts, even from the aching. It helped her ignore the frightening sounds outside, too.

The bed was so soft that Daphna stopped feeling it after a while. She was just sort of floating and counting. Floating and counting and breathing. Feather in. Feather out.

Finally, her eyes closed.

They snapped open.

The bed was shaking.

Daphna scrambled off it, ran to the wall, and fumbled the light on.

The bed was not shaking.

She was, though, with a pounding heart. She must have been dreaming. It was one a.m. Daphna turned the light back off and lay down again.

Eyes closed. Counting. In. Out. Feather breaths. Long, deep feather breaths. Daphna quickly found the rhythm that wafted her away from the world.

The bed started shaking again, but Daphna did not panic this time, since it was only her heart. She focused on her heart, thinking maybe that would calm it down. But, no, her heart was beating slowly, calmly.

Yet she was definitely shaking, even vibrating. She carefully put a hand on the mattress.

It was not vibrating.

It was *her.*

Daphna opened her eyes again.

She was no longer in the room.

Dexter lay in his bed staring at the ceiling, thinking about Nora. Once again, he saw her in that chamber under the museum pulling the red Mason's mask off her father's face and then struggling with him over the Book of the Living. *She* was the one who figured out it was him. *She* was the one who put her life on the line. It played over and over in his mind like an instant replay, but no matter how hard he tried to change the scene, she vanished with her father every time his crazy six bladed knife scraped their names off the page. And now they were gone. In Heaven he hoped. Safe in Heaven. *Please.*

And now he saw another scene play and replay in his mind: the two of them on the museum bench waiting for the Masons to take them below. "You can kiss me now," Nora had said. She'd told him she wasn't going to die in there without ever having been kissed. And they'd leaned forward.

But their lips never met.

No matter how many times Dex replayed that scene, their lips never met. It was agony.

He loved her.

Dex didn't care how absurd it was. For the first time in his life, he found himself not wishing to be somebody else, but simply to be *with* somebody else. He wouldn't need to be able to read if she were his— if he were hers.

But Nora had only been in his life long enough to torture him by leaving it. It was no different than having been able to speak Words of Power. It was no different than having been able to read for a short while. It was no different from constantly climbing back from the brink of death only to find himself on another, even more precarious brink every time.

Outrage surged through Dexter's body. He tried to ride it out, but it only got worse. He tried to pray like Nora did. It worked like magic for her, but praying to a God who's gone, even if he can hear you—even if he can *see* you—just didn't work for Dexter since He wouldn't help no matter what. The rage continued to build until Dex could feel it in his very bones, making him tremble on his mattress.

Dex heard muffled voices outside his window, then a slamming door, but he didn't care. Let someone come try to get him tonight. He'd tear *them* limb from limb. Or Daphna was welcome to handle it, unless she'd already snuck out to go find her boyfriend, that phony who thinks you can love someone because she looked cute a million years ago the one time you saw her. She probably thought she loved him, too. There was plenty of proof that flattery got you anything you wanted from Daphna Wax. Just ask a Pop who needed her homework done.

Yeah, she was probably sneaking down the street right now.

Dex got up and went to the window to see if he could catch her in the act of ditching him.

Again.

Menacing shadows were creeping around on the street.

Daphna was probably long gone.

If that's what she wanted, he'd let her go.

Dex went and laid back down, slowly losing his grip on himself. *Nora!* he thought, trying by sheer force of will to see her again. *Nora! I'm going to bring you home. I'm going to find you, and I'm going to bring you home!*

Did Daphna imagine he was too stupid to notice how she'd tried to use his feelings for Nora to manipulate him for Quinn's sake? If it came down to it, Dex suddenly realized, she would choose Quinn over him. Love was about the *other* person, and Daphna's infatuation with Quinn was clearly about herself. He was a book-worshipping nerd whose father owned a bookshop for crying out loud. He was the male version of Daphna Wax—her true twin! She was in love with herself!

Maybe they *should* split up again. Daphna could worry about Quinn, and he could worry about Nora. It was safer that way, anyway—keeping their precious ribs apart.

Dex's body went cold as it sometimes did when he got nervous or emotional, and he began to shiver. Maybe he should take something mechanical apart. He tried that idiotic breathing, but only once, clenching his eyes shut so hard that his head shook and all kinds of weird colors surfaced in his mind's eye.

It was a waste of time. Dex opened his eyes and sat up. He was going to wreck the room.

But he was no longer in it.

CHAPTER TEN
Somewhere

Dexter was standing somewhere, somewhere dark. He squinted, trying to help his eyes adjust. Something suddenly brushed the top of his head. He swiped at his spiky hair, relieved to find nothing there, but then something brushed his cheek, something delicate but disturbing, like an insect's wing. Then it happened again, and then again. Panicking, Dex frantically swatted and swiped at whatever they were. It felt like he was running through cobwebs, though he wasn't moving.

There were too many now—he was being swarmed. Crouching, Dex covered his face, but when the panic subsided a bit, he realized he wasn't being stung. In fact, as far as he could tell, he wasn't being harmed at all. Tentatively, he stood back up. Now it felt like—Dex wasn't quite sure. It was almost like holding his hand over those electric balls at the science center that made your hair stand on end.

The storm passed and Dex found he could see a bit now: little fluttering shapes were streaming past him, but they were moving too quickly to be much more than a blur. Trying to make them out was like trying to read the pages of a—

Dex raised his hands into the flitting stream and managed to trap some of what was floating by.

When he looked at what he'd caught, he saw, to his astonishment, *letters*.

Dex opened his mouth to scream at the endless, unforgivable cruelty of the cosmos, but another storm of letters swirled toward him out of the darkness. Dex took a step back, but then he saw a large, more recognizable shape materialize out of the storm. It was a human shape, a human shape made of flowing letters, just a few types it seemed, and he knew what they were without seeing them clearly: A's and T's and C's and G's. The figure of flowing letters approached Dexter and drew him into a tender embrace.

Nora. It was Nora—somehow, *Nora.*

Dex, she said, releasing him. *Dex! I love you! I love you!*

"I love you too!"

Can you help me?

"How?" Dex pled. "Just tell me how. Where are we?"

My Resting Place. But I don't belong here. Not yet.

"I'll stay with you! *Here!*" Dex promised. "Just let me stay here with you. I don't care about anything else anymore!"

Dex, you are not fully here. And it's not safe. I am with him. In his library at the bottom of his hole. Your mother's Book is here. Both your mothers' Books, and—

"Whose library?" Dex demanded. "Who is it?"

He threatens to cast us all into the Realm of Dead Souls. He has access to it here.

"No!"

Listen to me, Dex. You have nine days to bring me home, to bring us all home. I want to come home. I had no life until I met you. I wasn't even really alive. I want to live, and to live with you in my life. You've given me a reason to have a life.

"Yes!" Dex cried. "Yes! Tell me what to do. I'm— We're going to find the Book of Letters, Daphna and me, and we're going to say the Name, and we're going to make God fix everything!"

Find the Grail, Nora said, *but you must not attempt the Name! You will die! Your soul will die!*

"But, my eyes," Dex protested. "I was able to read the First Tongue. If the Name looks the same—"

Please, Dex. Please do not take that risk. We cannot be together in the Realm of Dead Souls. There is nothing there.

"Then—then, we'll get the Grail and—and—I'll trade it. I'll trade it for you!"

Would you do that for me?

"Yes!"

"Then here is what you must do."

"Anything! Tell me!"

"He has The Book of the Living."

"But, how——?"

"It was delivered to him. I don't know by who—but listen, Dex. The important thing is that he has it, and he has the means of adding names to it."

"I'll give him the Grail, and he'll add you back!"

"I love you, Dex."

Dex reached out for Nora's flowing letters again. He tried to embrace her, but she pushed him gently away.

"No! Please," Dex begged. "I don't want to go yet!"

Nine days, Nora said. *Come for me in His library, Dex. You are my hope—my hero."*

"Nora!"

But the Letters that were Nora were drifting apart and floating away.

Moments later they were gone, and the darkness with them.

Dexter was back in the sad and broken world.

Daphna sat up slowly, unable to see clearly in what looked like a foggy sort of half-light. She rubbed her eyes, trying to clear it away.

Daphna, someone said.

"Quinn!"

Daphna jumped off the bed. There was no bed. She was—somewhere. But Quinn! Quinn was here!

She saw him.

He was there, coming toward her! She was in the Light! Daphna ran to Quinn and leapt into his arms. He was there and not there, but he caught her and spun her round. He spun her round and round and round, and she willed him not to stop—never, ever to stop.

But Quinn stopped. He set her down, looking grave.

Daphna reached up and brushed the curl away from his eye. She took his face in her hands and, on her tiptoes, kissed him. Quinn kissed her back, and to-gether they turned round again, slowly now, kissing and spinning in the Light.

But Quinn broke their embrace again. *Daphna,* he said.

"Are—are you okay?" Daphna asked, coming to her senses. Now she saw that there were no Books in the Light, not a single one. And the Light itself—it wasn't right. And Quinn's eyes were not emerald green, like an angel's. He was robed in white, but he did not have wings. "Is—Are you—?" she asked. "This is Heaven, not Purgatory, isn't it? There is no Purgatory, right?"

Quinn nodded. *This is Heaven,* he said, *but I am not fully here, and neither are you. Come.* He took her hand and began shepherding her through the faded Light.

"So you're not—?"

I'm in a coma, still in Mr. Brown's operating room. Dr. Lewis is with me, but I don't know how long it will be before people find us there.

"What happened here?" Daphna asked, looking around again as she was lead on. It seemed to her that the dimness around her was due to some kind of smoke suspended in the Light. But now shapes were beginning to materialize around her. Daphna hurried forward, hoping to shorten the time before she was once again among the Sacred Books, one of which was *her* Book, the resting place of her soul.

But now Daphna could see.

She stopped cold, aghast.

It was her nightmare.

The shelves—the infinite shelves of Heaven's eternal library—had been all but demolished. All she could see, for as far as she could see, was nothing but smoldering black husks.

Worse, they were barren.

It was the most desolate scene Daphna had ever beheld. "The Books?" she choked. "Have they all been—?"

Quinn pulled Daphna on. There was no need to weave through the maze of shelves, for a massive swath of destruction had been scorched right through the mutilated stacks. They passed a pile of Books with keys in their covers, all laying open. Daphna was too harrowed even to acknowledge them.

Soon enough, they passed beyond the ruination—or so Daphna thought. Yet now she stopped short again, horrified anew. She could not have conceived of anything worse than the decimated shelves—yet here was worse.

Here were the B ooks, millions upon millions of

Books, heaped in a slowly smoldering pile, the top of which she could not take in. It was a towering mountain of burning Books. Was hers among them? Would that mean her soul could never rest?

Books slid off the mountain even as they burned, and many fell open in the diminished Light around it. Daphna could see the letters streaming across their pages, the letters man knew as DNA. They were turning to dust and rising off the pages like—

Smoke.

That was what was darkening the Light.

Daphna wretched.

Quinn pointed. Angels were moving solemnly but swiftly around the mountain, lifting Books off with quivering translucent hands. They dripped large tears on each one as they rushed them away, trying to salvage souls.

It was looking for a particular Book, Quinn said. *The Dragon.*

"The Book of Letters."

Quinn nodded. *But he was convinced it's not here.*

"Jesus," Daphna said. "We think he stole it."

The angels told him that, Quinn explained, *to stop the burning.*

"Then—he really did steal it?"

The angels only know for sure that the Book vanished when Jesus left Heaven. They don't know if he stashed it on a hidden shelf before returning to Earth—because he never came back.

"He never came back to Heaven—after the forty days?"

Never.

"Then he did read the Name wrong!"

They have no way of knowing, so they searched the shelves. It's all they could do.

"Mr. Brown thinks the book is in the Realm of Dead Souls," Daphna said. "That's where he had Dr. Lewis try to send you."

The Dragon does not think so, Quinn replied. *When the angels directed its attention to the world, it sensed the book was there. That's when it began to attack the border.*

"My mother, and Evelyn, and Wren, and Dr. Fludd—Nora—" Daphna couldn't hold back the questions anymore. She had to know.

The Dragon, Quinn said, turning to her with sad, pleading eyes. He seemed unable to hold his emotions in check any longer as well. *It took them!* he cried. *In their Books! It took them in their Books. My parents, too. It took all their Books!*

Daphna looked up again at the mountain of smoking souls as the sheer magnitude of what had happened seeped into her heart.

They are in his Library now, Quinn groaned. *And it's my fault! I sent my parents here. I erased them from the Book of the Living. I have to bring them back. You have to help me get them back before it's too late!*

"Quinn, you always expect the best!" Daphna cried. "I need your optimism! Tell me what to do! I'll do anything!

I don't know what it wants, Quinn said, getting a measure of control back, *but I have heard the angels say that it dares not confront the world of the living, not while the Book of Letters exists. It wants to have the Book, to possess it—to use it.*

"We'll find it!" Daphna promised. "Dex and I will find it, and we will use it!"

Daphna, Quinn said, his gorgeous eyes steady and strong holding hers. *You will not be able to speak the Name. You will die if you try. Your soul will shrivel and die, and we will never be together.*

"But—!"

There is a way. A terrible way.

"Quinn! Tell me!"

The angels believe that if the book were destroyed, he who destroyed it would perish with it.

"Then we have no hope!"

But we do: The Red Dragon himself has the power to destroy the book.

"But—how—?"

The Dragon's tongue. Its language. Its words—

Its fire!

Yes.

Daphna sputtered as the enormity of the task Quinn was asking her to take on sank in. "We have to find it," she whimpered, "and *take it to him?* When *that's exactly what he wants?"*

There is no other way. You must take the Grail down into his pit.

"Can you help me?"

I will try. If you can come to me again. I can try. I love you.

"I love you too."

Quinn began gently moving Daphna back through the smoke-choked Light.

"The Red Dragon," Daphna whined as she felt herself returning to herself. *"What is it?"*

Surely you know, Quinn said. There was only his voice now.

"Yes," Daphna admitted. "I know."

But before she could force herself to name the beast, she found herself back in bed.

CHAPTER ELEVEN
Simple as That

"It's called Projection—Astral Projection. I think it's like what we did with the Aleph, but different. Boy, I wish we still had that book."

"What?" Dex's eyes were open. That was not Nora's voice. It was his sister's, and he could not help but sigh, bitterly.

"Happy to see you too."

Dex sat up to find Daphna sitting on his desk, reading her cell phone. "What time is it?" he asked.

"Six. Listen to this—it's Wikipedia. I know it's not the best source because it's not exactly full of peer-reviewed entries like a truly reliable—"

"Who cares, Daphna!"

"Anyway, listen: 'Astral projection, or astral travel, is an interpretation of any form of out-of-body-experience (OBE) that assumes the existence of an 'astral body' separate from the physical body and capable of traveling outside it. Astral projection or travel denotes the astral body leaving the physical body to travel in the astral plane.'"

Dex, still groggy and disappointed to be back in the "real" world, was having trouble processing any of this. "How—?" he started to ask, but Daphna kept reading.

"'The idea of astral travel is rooted in common worldwide religious accounts of the afterlife in which the consciousness' or soul's journey or "ascent" is described in such terms as 'an out-of-body experience,' wherein the spiritual traveler leaves the physical body and travels in his or her subtle body (or dream body or astral body) into 'higher' realms.' It is therefore associated with near death experiences and is also frequently reported as spontaneously experienced in association with sleep and dreams, illness, surgical operations, drug experiences, sleep paralysis, and forms of meditation.'"

"Daphna," Dex said, finally feeling his mind beginning to clear. "I don't understand how you—"

"It happened to me too. I talked to Quinn. He's alive, in a coma, but his soul is in Heaven. I came in this morning to tell you and heard you telling Nora that you love her, and I could tell you weren't just talking in your sleep. I was waiting for you to come back."

Dex flushed with embarrassment, then anger.

"I told Quinn I love him too," Daphna said. And before Dex could say anything back, she clicked on her screen and said, "Listen to this. I found it searching, 'Communicating with Angelic Beings': 'It's been well established by Quantum Physics that all forms of existence—even energy forms otherwise invisible to the human eye—have a measurable vibrational frequency.'"

Dex, now fully awake, was nonetheless still baffled. "What's that got to do with—?"

"Remember when Dr. Fludd told us, or me anyway, about our ribs? In her office?"

Dex did remember. "She said for some reason they vibrate."

"So listen to this: 'Angels have a higher, purer vibrational frequency than humans. But with practice, typically years of meditation, a person can refine their frequency until it matches those of angels. Consequently, they can 'tune in' to the angelic realm. This is very much like receiving a private radio signal or subscribing to a restricted satellite channel.'"

"We can do it," Dex said, thrilled. "Our ribs let us do it!"

Daphna nodded, her eyes wide. "We've just never tried before. I mean, why would we have? And I'm betting that since Nora and Quinn aren't really angels, it was easier to match their frequencies."

Dex immediately lay back down and closed his eyes. Daphna made no objection, but rather just watched him in silence. After a few minutes, he opened them again.

"I couldn't do it this morning, either," she said.

Dex threw off his covers and sat up again. Like his sister, he'd not changed out of the jeans and store T-shirt he'd put on last night. He even had his shoes on.

Ready to run at all times.

"Dex," Daphna said, her voice now wavering, "the Books in Heaven—so many—millions! They were burned! Piled up in a mountain as high as—a burning mountain, Dex! We have to find the Book of Letters! Quinn told me that it—the Dragon—it won't do anything here until it gets it. It's afraid, I bet, of someone finding it and summoning God. I think it wants to do that itself—what?"

"That's really good," Dex said, "except for one thing."

"What?"

"Nora told me that he somehow got The Book of the Living." Dex hesitated to share the rest, but Daphna was as desperate as he was. "And she said that if we take him the Grail, he'll trade with us. I know that sounds crazy," he added before Daphna could tell him so, "but she also said he has a way to write in it. I know he'll do something terrible if we give him the—"

"Perfect."

"What other choice to we have, Daphna?"

"I said, that's perfect."

"It is?"

"Quinn told me that anyone who destroys the Book of Letters would die. And that the Red Dragon's fire can do it. So—"

"We make the trade, figure out how to get the names back into the Book of the Living, then get him to destroy the Grail before he uses it to destroy the world."

"Right."

"Simple as that," Dex said, pretending it wasn't as absurd as it sounded.

"So now all we need to do is find the Grail," Daphna said, also refusing to face the hopelessness of their situation. "Then climb down into a hellhole and take it to—his library, I guess."

"I was with Nora," Dex said, "in—she called it her Resting Place. She was—It was all a blur of letters—"

"Oh, my God," Daphna gasped. "Her *Book*. You were in her Book! The Book that houses her soul!"

"Nora says he's going to cast it into the Realm of Dead Souls. Mom's and Evelyn's Books too. He has access to it."

"Oh, my God!" Daphna cried. "We need to find

the Grail. We need to find it now!"

"Did you find any new theories about where it might be?"

"Tons," Daphna said, trying to calm down. "So I think we might be better off learning more about how to contact Quinn and Nora again—to get more help from them. I was worried I might have just gotten lucky last night, so I did a search about it."

"And?"

"I didn't find anything too helpful online, but there's a book that sounds perfect called, 'Celestial Frequencies: How to Talk to Angels.' There's one copy down at the Central Library. I didn't put it on hold, but maybe I ought—"

Daphna looked down at her computer and frowned. She tapped some keys. "It's offline," she complained. "Connection's broken."

Just then the light in the room went out.

"Uh, oh," Dex said. "Think it's just us?" He moved to the window behind the desk to look outside. Daphna helped him sweep the curtains apart.

Neither could believe their eyes.

CHAPTER TWELVE
The Real Deal

All the houses the twins could see had their front doors either standing open or knocked down, and just about every visible bottom floor window was shattered. Furniture, evidently thrown out of windows, lay like broken sculptures on all the front lawns. There was a recliner actually sitting on top of a car in someone's driveway, one leg through the sunroof.

Weirdly, and disturbingly, books were scattered all around. They were on the grass, the sidewalks, even the streets.

It looked like it had rained books.

"What—but—" Daphna stuttered. "How could—?"

"We didn't hear anything," Dex said. "When we were gone—We must have been completely out of it." The degree to which they'd been vulnerable—defenseless—made him feel retroactively terrified.

"But, why not our house?"

Dex pressed his face to the window, trying to see the driveway, but the angle was too sharp. There was no furniture on their lawn as far as he could tell. "We better go see," he decided.

The twins hurried fearfully downstairs. Dr. Fludd's furniture all appeared to be where it was yesterday. Books were in their places on the shelves.

Hesitantly, Dexter opened the front door.

"*Dex,*" Daphna whispered before he stuck his head outside, "if we're sure we're going to get killed—blown up or something—"

"We'll separate."

"But only—"

"If we're sure. I got it. It makes sense."

Dex peeked outside. When nothing happened, he took a few steps through the door. Daphna followed, cringing.

The house hadn't been spared, not entirely. A

car, a compact convertible sports car, had been driven partway into the garage, right through the heavy metal door, the left side of which was bent around it.

Dex and Daphna slowly approached the car, both thinking that anyone could be in it, or in the garage—or the house! They could have been murdered in their sleep!

The car was empty.

"Look," Dex said, pointing at the ground.

A trail of blood led from the driver's side door back toward the sidewalk.

"They got hurt and ran off?" Daphna guessed.

"Maybe," Dex said, looking into the driver's seat. "But I don't see blood in here."

"How could that be?"

Dex followed the trail to where it ended at the curb. "Maybe he didn't start bleeding until he got out of the car. Or maybe someone dragged him out and beat him up. He must've gotten into another car and left."

"Why didn't anyone come into the house?" Daphna asked. "This clearly wasn't the work of one person." She waved at the street. "More like a marauding horde." What if she'd gone out last night and gotten caught up in it?

"Is the electricity out?"

The twins scanned the street. From what they could see, nothing electrical seemed to be on in anyone's houses, but it was hard to be sure. Daphna hurried to the garage door panel on the side of the house to see if it was on. The numbers didn't beep when she pushed them. "It's dead," she said. "But hold on." She checked her phone. "This is working," she said. "It's really not good that yours is lost."

"I consider it good that Nora taking it saved my life," Dex said. "Anyway, let's maybe figure out what's going on from inside the house."

"Good idea."

Dexter crawled under the mangled garage door, so Daphna went in behind him, and they hurried into the kitchen.

Daphna sat down at the table and started searching the web while Dex raided the fridge, this time with at least a little restraint. He took out some cheese, a bunch of fruit, and what was left of the ravaged cold cuts, then brought it all over to the table.

"There are videos all over the web of fighting in the streets," Daphna said. "I think it's really bad in Israel. But I want to see what's happening—here's a local news site." She set the phone inside a Lucite napkin holder, so they could watch it hands-free.

Dex sat down and crammed a bunch of roast beef into his mouth. He was turning into a savage.

A clip was already playing on the website, a livestream it seemed. More riots, but this time it was America. In fact, it looked like—

"That's the library!" Daphna cried, nearly choking on a strawberry she'd shoved into her mouth whole.

The Central Library was on screen. People were running out of it with armloads of books, only to be attacked by others the moment they emerged, evidently for their books. People were at the windows, tossing books out. A car-carrier was on the sidewalk—actually partway up onto the front steps. It had evidently been used to reach the lower windows, but now people were on top of it, tipping the vehicles off.

An exhausted looking newscaster came on from his studio. "Similar scenes," he said, "are taking place at libraries around the world, at libraries and bookstores, and anywhere else books are found. All of this has been attributed to a video, now gone viral, shot secretly here in Portland at OHSU by a nurse. If you have not seen it yet—here it is again."

Another video came on, this one shot in a hospital room. A small, pale man was sitting on a bed in those hideous pajamas they make you wear.

"Picker!" the twins both shouted at the screen.

They were amazed to see the little man who'd temporarily had his hands on the Book of Nonsense at the city dump. They thought he'd been killed there in what now felt like another lifetime. He looked sick and shriveled, but was him. It was definitely him.

"That's it?" Picker said to the screen. "A phone?"

"Hurry," a female voice whispered, evidently the nurse's. She must have been holding the phone, which was shaking a bit. "The cameras they brought in before—" she said, "it was all fake. They recorded it, but they aren't going to show it to anyone. They think they're the only people who should know what's really going on. But I don't. I'm going to put this on the web. The whole world will be able to see it." It sounded like she swallowed a sob before adding, "They're always trying to cover things up around here. But people have a right to know what's happening, no matter how bad it is!"

"All right then. Good. That's more like it."

"Tell them what you told Dr. Brody."

"Okay, right. Okay." Picker straightened his pajamas a bit. "How do I look?" he asked. "Never mind. HOW DO YOU LIKE ME NOW?"

"Mr. Picarelli," the nurse urged. "*Please*. I don't know how long—"

"Okay, okay. Here's the deal, people. Listen up, 'cause the Devil's in the details." Picker laughed at this, a hacking, coughing sort of high-pitched, childish laugh. "Sorry," he said. "My bad. Anyway, so like I was saying, here's the deal: LIFE AS YOU KNOW IT IS OVER!" He shouted this last part with his nostrils flaring, then broke up laughing again.

"*Mr. Picarelli!*"

"Sorry," he said, again, recovering. "Right. Sorry. Here's the deal—the *real deal*: The Desolator has returned to rule what is rightfully his: meaning, you." Picker broke into yet another laugh. He looked thrilled, transported. "AND I'VE BEEN PICKED!" he crowed. "ME! PICKER! I've been picked to tell you that he will soon be among you, and that only some of you will be allowed to stay. AND GUESS WHO GETS TO PICK, YOU LOUSY JERKS!" Picker beamed then, like a child offered his choice of gifts from a store full of toys. "Okay, not me," he admitted. "But still, I might get a say, and I have my own special collection job, so YOU MIGHT WANT TO PAY A LITTLE RESPECT!"

Once again, there was an audible sob from the nurse holding the camera, which she almost dropped. The floor tiles came on screen for a moment.

"The Book of Names!" Daphna cried. "It was him! He somehow got it from the Masons and took it to the Dragon!"

"Now," Picker said when the Nurse had him back on camera, "there is one more thing. There's a certain *book*. He would like to have this certain book before he makes his grand entrance. It's a golden book with a key in it. Trust me, you'll know it if you see it, unless its cover has been disguised, which it probably has. So the book could be anywhere, even in your own house! But you'll know it the moment you touch it—trust me on this. The Red Dragon needs a viceroy, and the one who brings him the Golden Book will serve at his side. But trust me folks, you do NOT want to open the book. Anyone who opens it will be made an example of—an example to last all time, meaning forever. He picked me to tell you this. SO HOW DO YOU LIKE—!"

The video cut out, and the news came back on.

"Officials at OHSU call the video a hoax perpetrated by a disgruntled employee," the newscaster explained, "who has since been fired. But many—millions it seems—are not so quick to dismiss these incredible claims, given the nature of the current crisis." He paused a moment as an awful twitch took hold of his face, twisting it up around his left eye.

"He's barely controlling himself," Dex said.

"The patient, Arthur Picarelli," the newscaster continued when the tic passed, "had been in a coma for nearly a year, having been injured in a bizarre accident at the Metro Central Dump. You may recall the apparent collapse there, which was never satisfactorily explained. It is nearly unprecedented for a patient in Mr. Picarelli's condition to regain consciousness, let alone the ability to speak so soon. The Pope himself has even weighed in on the matter, refusing to discount the possibility that the Devil is now among us. His coming, a Vatican spokesperson suggested, may have been signaled by the bizarre meteorological events. You may also recall the Church made no such allowances during the plague scare, when similar rumors circulated around the world. Church authorities strongly urge people to remain calm, and to pray. Nonbelievers, they warn, may not get another chance to—THAT'S IT!" the newscaster suddenly roared.

He pushed his chair back, but before he got up, he touched his ear, then said, "We—Yes, the President is ready to address the nation." After two deep breaths, he added, "We understand that electricity is out all over the Greater Portland area because of rioting at power stations, but we will continue to broadcast this livestream as long as we can. Here is the President of the United States of America."

The President came on from the Oval Office. This time he was standing in front of his desk wearing a dark blue suit and a crimson tie. It looked like he'd shaved a bit too quickly; there were a few nicks on his cheek.

But he didn't look insane or about to go insane, which comforted the twins immensely.

"Greetings, my fellow Americans," he said. "It seems only hours ago that I spoke to you during a similarly frightening and bewildering time. I'd like to remind you that cooler heads prevailed even while the plague was undeniably spreading. Millions of folks did not act on rumors, fears, superstitions, or mistrust. We assured you that we would come up with a cure for the disease, and that is exactly what we did. Dr. Roberta Fludd, the national hero who led the team that devised the cure, is heading up a task force working to bring this new situation under control. We know that we are in most capable hands."

The twins shook their heads.

"And so we must ask for your patience and restraint once again while we ascertain the true nature of these weather anomalies. I am pleased to report that worldwide temperatures are slowly returning to normal, though it is still dangerously hot in many places. It is simply not safe to be outside. And because of the effect this crisis is having on people, for the safety of all our citizens, I have signed an official order authorizing Martial Law. An immediate twenty-four hour curfew is under effect nationwide while our team of top scientists, led by the genius Dr. Fludd, investigates the meteor strike in Portland, Oregon. Only authorities have clearance to be on the road or in the air. We do not anticipate this curfew extending beyond seventy-two hours, by which time we intend to put this matter to rest. Please remain by your TV's, radios, and computer screens for regular updates. Thank you and God bless America."

The local newscaster returned, looking sweaty but a bit more composed. "We are unable to bring you any footage of what is already being referred to on the Internet as 'Hellmouth,'" he said, "the crater created by the impact of the so-called meteor that touched down in Gabriel Park. This is the best image we have. It was taken by a digital camera mounted on a viewer's drone before it was destroyed."

"Hellmouth?" Daphna gasped. The name was not a surprise upon reflection, but it horrified her, anyway.

One more video came on, a shaky sky scene. The view kept shifting from city streets to houses to clouds and back again. But for a few moments it settled, and the twins' both performed double takes. There, in the distance, under circling military jets, was Gabriel Park—or what used to be Gabriel Park. What was there instead was a gaping hole the size of a dozen city blocks, spewing black and mustard-colored smoke. The view dipped a bit, showing hundreds of police and military vehicles ringing the hole, but then there was a flash of red and the video cut out.

The studio came back on, but the newscaster was no longer in his seat. There was shouting and the sound of things breaking. The camera began to shake.

Daphna closed the browser, then shoved the phone into her pocket. She slumped down next to her brother, who was still eating.

"I was going to say, now I have nowhere to go when I skip school," Dex said. "But then I remembered I have nowhere to go to school."

Daphna didn't reply to this. She felt utterly defeated. It was too much. It was all just too much even to comprehend. "That was the park falling on our heads outside," she finally said. *"Hellmouth,* Dex!"

"I must admit that doesn't sound very inviting."

The Devil, Daphna thought. *There wasn't supposed to be a Devil!* Her father—*Adam himself!*—had told them so. He and Eve had been talked into reading from The Book of Knowledge by the snake, but that had been Lilit, who was devilish enough. How could God not have told his first creations that there was something so evil in the world? *And something even worse!* Daphna closed her eyes and began the feather breathing. *Quinn!* she called out in her mind. *Quinn!* But it was no use. She opened her eyes to see Dexter trying to reach Nora. When he opened his eyes, it was obvious he'd had no luck, either.

"We need help," Daphna declared. "We need to get that book about talking to angels at the library. We need to learn how to contact Quinn and Nora again. They'll know how to help us."

"Then let's get going, already," Dex said. He stood up and looked at the door to the garage as if they were going to leave that very moment. But at that very moment, the blade of an axe chopped through it.

CHAPTER THIRTEEN
Twisted

The twins screamed. But both remained where they were—Dex on his feet, Daphna sitting down—too stunned to move.

The axe was ripped out of the door, which was then kicked open to reveal an unshaven middle-aged man in a red bathrobe, grinning like a psycho. The twins still didn't move, even when he took a step into the kitchen. But then there was bang, and suddenly he was face down on the floor, bleeding from his back. Someone had shot him.

Finally, the twins reacted.

They ran for the front door, but no sooner did they reach it, they backed away. The knob was rattling. Through the tall, skinny windows on either side of the door, they saw a crowd of people, some of whom saw them back. Now many fists were pounding the door.

It burst open just as Dex and Daphna reached the den. They scrambled past the leather couches and massive wall-mounted TV. People were chasing them. They sprinted through a sitting room, then the dining room.

"Back steps!" Dex cried. There was a set of steps to the second floor back there. They scrambled up them, stumbling along the way.

"What's happening?" Daphna wailed, looking back for a moment from the top of the steps. Two people appeared at the bottom, a man and a woman, both wielding garden tools.

Dex looked around wildly, trying to decide what to do, but Daphna grabbed him by the arm and dragged him down the hall into Dr. Fludd's bedroom. Once inside, she slammed the door. There was no lock, so they used a dresser to block it. They'd only just gotten it into place before the rattling and pounding began.

"What are you doing?" Dex cried after looking around the room. "We're trapped!" He ran to the window. There were people in the backyard now, dozens of them. Normal people who wanted to kill someone. Fortunately, they seemed to be trying to kill each other at the same time they were trying to get into the house.

"Dex!" Daphna shouted. "Dex!"

When Dex looked back, he saw Daphna pointing to a small, square door set into the wall next to the bed.

The pounding on the bedroom door was juttering the dresser. Dex rushed over and stabilized it. "Oh!" he said, looking back at that little door. Dr. Fludd had shown it to them on their 'Grand Tour.' "Dumbwaiter!"

Daphna had it open. Now she was ripping the comforter off the bed. "Help me!" she cried. "The serving box is up above!"

Dex left the dresser to its fate. Moments later, the door behind it splintered loudly.

The axe.

Together the twins stuffed the comforter into the chute and let it fall. They grabbed pillows and stuffed them down after it.

The door crashed in with the axe stuck in it. A man with a giant mustache yanked it out, then started shoving the dresser aside.

"Jump!" Dexter cried. "Watch the cable!"

Daphna, shaking, climbed into the hole feet first. Instead of jumping, she started crab-walking down the shaft, gripping the cable with one hand.

Dex went in head first after her, ready to dive down the chute, but his sister was only halfway down. When he grabbed the cable to stop himself, someone grabbed his ankle.

He was being pulled back up.

"It's clear down here!" Daphna called up from below. She'd let herself fall the last few feet and landed awkwardly, but softly. "Hurry!"

Dex's hands flailed around, smacking the chute's walls, but they managed to find the cable again. He stopped himself from being hauled back into the room, at least for a moment.

Now Dexter's ankle was being twisted round, but

before he was forced to let go of the cable, an awful grunt sounded from above, and then his ankle was free. Dex lurched further forward into the chute, pulling his legs in behind him. Then he shimmied down onto it, afraid to let himself fall now that he saw how far it was. Though his hands were wet with sweat, he was able to hold on with legs clenched around the cable and inch his way down to the bottom.

The moment she could, Daphna yanked her brother out of the chute onto the kitchen floor. No one was there but the man who'd been shot in the back chopping down the door from the garage, and he lay face down, unmoving.

Footsteps were pounding their way.

Dex leapt to his feet. He jumped directly over the body into the garage, then scrambled into the Hummer and started it up, grateful for his foresight with the keys.

Daphna ran after him but could not bring herself to jump over a corpse. When she heard the Hummer roar to life, she understood what Dex was doing, but there was no way she was making that jump.

"Find the books!" someone yelled. People were streaming into the house.

There was shooting again.

Her wobbling knees could barely support her, but Daphna forced herself to take a giant step over the dead man with her eyes closed. Her front foot came down beyond him, only just, but the dead man—Not dead!—turned on his side and grabbed her other ankle as it passed over him.

Daphna screamed and yanked it free.

Then she scrambled up into the Hummer next to her brother. "Go!" she cried, smacking the door lock button. But then she felt her pocket. "My phone!" she realized. "It must have fallen out in the chute! Forget it," she decided, though Dex hadn't responded. "Go! Go! Go!"

Dex was eying the little sports car and the twisted metal garage door partly on top of it. They didn't look like much of a problem. The Hummer was a tank, but he was worried. "What if someone's out there?" he asked, craning to see.

"JUST GO!" Daphna wailed. People, *killers*, were coming into the garage now from the kitchen. There was a woman in a yellow dress with an armload of Dr. Fludd's books, but right behind her was a hulking, bear of a man waving a gun.

Dex put the car in gear and floored it. The twins both flew back in their seats.

The Hummer simply crushed the back end of the little car, sending the twins momentarily up into the roof of the monster truck. The impact with the garage door sent it flying. They slammed onto the driveway, which was clear of people, then into the street. Dex slammed the brakes to avoid driving them right into the houses across the way. A dozen people were on the sidewalk, and they all scattered when the Hummer nearly ran them down.

Now Dex backed off the sidewalk and got them aimed in the right direction. The mob gave chase, but it was no use.

With tires squealing, the Hummer sped away.

CHAPTER FOURTEEN
Overdue

Dexter crashed over the corner onto Dosch, then went right through a red light, turned left, and headed up the hill back toward the high school. Abandoned vehicles littered the road, but he just barged right through them, knocking them aside like toys.

Daphna, to her brother's surprise, hadn't said a word since they'd left the garage. Finally, she spoke, but all she said was, "Keep going straight—straight to downtown."

Dex nodded, keeping his eyes focused on the road. It was incredible, but his vision wasn't giving him the slightest problem this time. Of course, not worrying about crashing made it considerably easier to navigate. "You were trying to contact him," he realized. That's why she'd been so quiet.

"I can't do it anymore," Daphna said, sounding distraught. "We have to get to the library and find that book to teach us how!" She tried to breathe.

"What about the news? There are guys there with guns."

"Maybe they'll be gone, because of the Martial Law."

"*Like those fine upstanding folks we just had over for tea?*"

"Don't yell at me, Dexter!"

"I'm not yelling!" Dex tried to breathe. He'd noticed that when he breathed in through his nose, he could also draw air down through his throat. Or it felt like he could. It seemed like a lot more oxygen flooded his system that way, which helped.

"Maybe the underground tunnels connect to the library," Daphna said. "Maybe we can sneak in."

Dex had no desire to go traipsing around under the city again, but it sounded better than facing madmen with guns.

They were passing the high school. Daphna

glanced dejectedly at the remains, which were still on fire. No one was there to fight the flames. "Let's just get downtown without killing anyone," she said, "especially ourselves."

Dexter had them moving swiftly now, but he was forced to weave around abandoned vehicles once he left Hillsdale behind. With his lousy depth perception, he clipped almost every one. The Hummer didn't complain, and neither did Daphna. She directed him to stay right when the road split, and then they headed toward the Waterfront.

When they came alongside the river, he had to drive on the shoulder, which slowed them at times almost to a crawl. Twice he had to nudge minivans out of the way to get past—but they were getting there. Not many people were on these streets, and the few they saw were all busy looting cars.

"Okay," Daphna said, "take a left and head toward Tenth. We'll be right near, Quinn."

"Ah, Daphna—"

"Don't start with me, Dexter! I told you he's still in a coma!"

"We're being followed."

"What?"

"By someone famous I think."

Daphna jerked around in her seat. She recognized the white stretch SUV instantly, though now it was severely dented and scraped. The driver was a grim-looking man dressed in black. The older man sitting next to him had white hair falling down the sides of his otherwise bald head like a curtain. She could see his sad eyes honing in on them.

"It's them!" Daphna cried. "It's *him!* The Secret Keeper! They're going to kill us! TAYLOR STREET! *TURN!*"

Dexter managed to make the turn, knocking aside one of those tiny little gas-saving cars. He'd often had the impulse to smash one of those.

He jammed on the breaks.

The street was completely blocked. Cars were everywhere, even up on the sidewalks.

"Dex, they're coming!"

The stretch SUV was making its way through the traffic behind them, bashing cars out of its way just as effectively as they had. Fortunately, it couldn't manage to get by the snarl a few hundred yards back.

It stopped.

Doors opened and half a dozen men dressed in black, all armed, jumped out. They didn't immediately charge the Hummer, though, but rather scanned the area around their truck. There were people on the street scavenging through cars there, but they all ducked out of sight. A few others were running in and out of broken storefronts with stolen goods in their arms.

But now the men in black turned their attention to the twins.

"Dex! We need to run!"

Daphna had her hand on the door, but before she opened it, Dexter hit the accelerator. The Hummer charged forward, crashing into the two cars ahead of it, two compacts. Both twins cried out at the impact, but Dex did not let up on the gas. There was the sound of breaking glass, of metal being crushed, and then they were moving again.

Moving *up*.

They were climbing over the cars.

Dex was so amazed that he stopped, and they just stayed there, teetering a bit on the roofs and trunks of the flattened compacts beneath them.

The Secret Keeper's men were sprinting toward them now. "Go!" Daphna shouted, regaining her senses. "Drive!"

Dex drove.

The Hummer slammed down over the compacts, mashing their hoods, then rolled up onto the next set of cars. He paused again, then drove again.

They were driving on top of the traffic.

But they weren't driving quickly enough. The men in black were weaving in and out of the gridlock quickly, gaining ground.

"Dex," Daphna urged, twisting round to see them, "just floor it!"

Dex floored it.

The Hummer leaped up onto the next set of cars, mangling them just like he'd seen in those crash-up derbies on TV. Then they were overtop more. The twins were tossed violently about in their seats, but they were moving quickly now.

"It's on Tenth," Daphna said when she saw they'd put some distance between themselves and the men in black. "Two more blocks," she added. "BUS!"

Just before they hit the back of the empty Trimet bus, Dex swerved to the right, sending them crashing down off the cars they'd been demolishing. The sidewalk was clear just there, so Dex barreled down it, mowing down metal signs along the way. The Hummer was taking a terrible beating, but didn't seem the slightest bit discouraged.

"Tenth! Turn!"

Dexter turned, then hit the brakes again.

So much for Martial Law.

A dozen armed men were in front of the library, none of them cops. They were standing guard while dozens of other men inside threw books out of windows. Thousands of books swamped the front steps and sidewalks. No one noticed the twins.

"Dex," Daphna said, glancing behind them. "I know where that angel book is, or where it should be, anyway." There was no sign of the Secret Keeper's men yet. "There," she said, turning round again, pointing, "on the third floor. See the first square window over the arched ones? It's in there. Well, there, but towards the other side of the building."

"Is there a tunnel entrance around here?"

Daphna looked back once again. "I don't think we have time for tunnels."

"Then how are we going—?"

"Look at that."

It took a moment for Dex to realize what Daphna was pointing to. "You've got to be kidding me."

Daphna was pointing at the car-carrier they'd seen on the news. It was halfway up the library's front steps, now empty of cars.

"I'm not sure I can aim well enough," Dex said.

Daphna looked at the carrier. She looked at her brother, who was clearly willing to try. "I can't put it on you every time," she said. "I'm way overdue."

"What?"

"Switch with me. They're coming." Daphna didn't wait for her brother to answer. She jumped down from her door and ran around the front of the Hummer. Dex had already moved over by the time she climbed into the driver's seat.

The men in black were picking their way around and over the cars just behind them now.

"Oh, God," Daphna said, looking down at the pedals. "I'm sorry. I don't even know what—"

Dexter reached his foot across and slammed down the accelerator. The Hummer roared ahead.

Daphna was shocked, but she had the wheel. The armed men guarding the library saw them now, but they were too surprised to react. Guns were eventually raised, but not before the Hummer hit the back of the carrier.

Arms rigid, elbows locked, Daphna held the wheel as best she could.

They raced up the carrier's back at full-speed.

When they went airborne, both twins closed their eyes.

And so neither saw the astonished faces of the guards as the giant but beaten up Hummer launched itself right over them and blasted its way amid a spray of broken bricks and exploding glass into the library.

The Hummer's side windows shattered as it landed inside the building. The twins opened their eyes to see books flying over the cracked windshield.

"Breaks!" Daphna shrieked.

Dexter slammed the brake, but the Hummer began to skid, bashing through shelves, sending them flying over their roof one after another along with the books they'd held. A computer screen hit the windshield, spider webbing it completely before bouncing up and away. They were crushing desks as well.

Daphna slammed her own foot down on top of her brother's.

The tires shrieked in protest as the Hummer fishtailed, launching more shelves and books every which way.

But then, at last, they stopped.

CHAPTER FIFTEEN
Desperate Steps

The twins remained where they were with their legs intertwined. The windshield was covered in books, blocking their view of the library.

It was quiet.

"Are we still alive?" Dex finally asked, "because I think I had a heart attack. Twelve, actually."

"I think so." Daphna put the Hummer in park and freed her leg.

"That was," Dex added, taking his leg back as well, "awesome. You did it."

"Yeah," Daphna said. "It kinda was. Thanks for the hand. Or the foot, I guess."

They opened their doors and climbed down. Books slid off the roof, landing on the books strewn everywhere across the floor. The hall was a complete shambles. Not a single shelf stood upright.

The twins turned and looked back across the library at the path of destruction they'd wreaked all the way from the gaping hole in the side of the building.

Gunfire sounded outside.

They dropped to the floor.

"We better hurry!" Daphna whispered as loudly as she dared.

"You'd *better hurry. How are you going to find anything in this mess?"*

"Just keep watch," Daphna said, crawling over to a heap of books to examine their spines. They were, at least, approximately similar in call numbers.

Dex got up as far as a crouch and hurried back to the broken wall, where he peeked through the glass shards and crushed bricks left around the window frame. "Daphna," he shouted, turning back to see his sister grabbing books up, checking their spines, and tossing them away as quickly as she could. "Only the Secret Keeper's men are down there now. Some are coming inside!"

On cue, gunshots rang out from inside the library.

Daphna now dug frantically through the books. "I need the 232's!" she cried.

"Hurry!"

"I'm trying!"

They could hear running in other halls. Gunshots and the reverberations of gunshots.

"Hurry!"

Someone yelled, "Secure the building!"

It dawned on Dexter that it wasn't especially helpful of him to just stand there shouting hurry. He ran back to the Hummer to get it started again.

"I found it!" his sister cried, leaping up with a book held over her head. "Let's go! Let's go!" She scrambled over to the Hummer and into the passenger seat next to her brother.

But when Dexter turned the key, it didn't start.

Men in black were there now, in the rear view mirror.

"Get us out of here!" Daphna wailed.

Dex worked the key again. Nothing. Then nothing again. "It won't start!"

It started.

Behind the Hummer, someone yelled, "Stop!"

In the rear view mirror, Dex saw half a dozen men in black aiming guns at them. He put the truck in reverse, hit the accelerator, and drove directly at them.

"Dex!"

The men leapt out of the way as the Hummer drove over books and fallen shelves and computer debris. Dex hit the brakes, shifted to forward, then turned toward a large set of wooden doors.

He rammed right through them.

"The steps!" Daphna cried.

There was a set of wide, etched granite steps winding down to the lower levels at the end of the open hall they'd entered. Dexter swung the wheel around and sent them careening down them, scraping the passenger side along the walls as they went screeching along. There was enough room for the Hummer, but only just. The steps wound round again, so Dex furiously worked the wheel to stay with them, scraping and sparking all the way, ripping down the banister as they went.

The steps fed into another open hall on the second floor.

"Behind us!" Daphna cried. "More steps!"

Dex turned and saw them. These were black granite, also etched with some kind of pattern. He fought the wheel, and the walls, and forced the Hummer round the turns until he was looking straight down the final flight, directly at the library's front doors.

"Go! Go! Go!" Daphna shouted, looking back.

They slammed down the steps, skidded a bit through the main entry hall past checkout stations and computer terminals, then broke through a row of doors into the front vestibule. A moment later, they burst through the main entrance. Looking back, Daphna caught a glimpse of a quote on the wall they'd just demolished. It said, "I have always imagined Paradise to be a kind of library."

"Where am I going?" Dex shouted as they slammed their way through the cars littering the entryway.

"Quinn!" Daphna cried. "Go down to the Park blocks—*that way!*"

Dex went the way his sister was pointing, crashing and smashing through anything and everything in their way.

"Right!"

Dex turned right onto Park, but had to drive up on the sidewalk again. "There's the Museum!" Daphna yelled as they barreled past it. Had they been there just yesterday? "The clinic is right—keep going—*Stop!*"

Dex stopped.

"He's in there!" Daphna was pointing to the wellness clinic. Her guilt for taking so long to get back here, her dire need to make sure Quinn was okay— it all flooded her at once, threatening to make her faint.

"Then let's go get him, already."

Daphna looked at her brother, full of gratitude she didn't have time to express. She unlocked the doors.

But just as quickly, Dexter locked them.

The Hummer had suddenly been surrounded by men in dark robes and masks—blue masks. They all held swords.

"Masons!" Dexter cried.

"We don't have it!" Daphna shrieked at them. "Picker got it! It's not our fault if you—!"

Before Daphna could finish her sentence, before the twins had time to properly panic, the ring of Masons surrounding the Hummer collapsed. They fell out of sight as suddenly as if trap doors had opened beneath them in the street. Stunned, the twins looked to each other for an explanation, but before they could guess what had happened, they were surrounded again.

And so they had an explanation: men in black, holding guns with silencers. The guns, having been fired at the Masons, were now leveled at the twins.

Who sighed.

Dex unlocked the Hummer's doors, and the Secret Keeper of the Church climbed inside.

CHAPTER SIXTEEN
No lie is of the Truth

"The boy is safe," the Secret Keeper promised, looking into Daphna's panicking eyes in the rearview mirror. "He is in stable condition. The doctor is still with him. Portable generator."

"I forgot about the electricity!" Daphna cried. Relieved beyond words, she glanced up and down the street to assess their situation. Dex was already doing the same. There were men in black guarding it from all angles. Some were even on the rooftops.

There was nothing they could do, so the twins just sat where they were looking at the men in black look back at them through the cracked-up windshield.

"You didn't have to worry about the Masons," Dex said without turning to face the Secret Keeper with his baggy face and droopy eyes and creepy white curtain of hair. "They were going to rip our tongues out—not our ribs. That might have worked out really well for you."

"These Masons came down from Seattle," the Secret Keeper said, ignoring this. "They were wondering why their Portland brethren seemed to have fallen off the map after making such a fuss about finding their long sought Book of the Living."

"It's gone," Daphna said, also without turning round.

"Yes, we know," the Secret Keeper said. "The odd little man from the video. These men found it under the museum, but they gave it to him in exchange for grand promises of power beyond even their wildest dreams. The fools made a deal with the Devil."

The twins exchanged a worried glance at this and sagged in their seats.

"How did they find us here?" Dex asked.

"The Masons everywhere know that you and your sister were involved in the discovery of the Book of the Living. After making their exchange, they set out to find you, no doubt to learn what you know about this golden book. I expect they hoped you could help them find it and use it themselves. They've been following you for quite a while now."

"The Church is protecting us," Dex realized, turning to his sister. "They've been protecting us since we left Mr. G's. From rioters, but also from the Masons. They distracted those kids when they were about to attack us. Then they ripped the guy off me on the street, after I got knocked off my bike. They're the reason no one raided our house last night, and when those nutcases got in today, they protected us there, too. I bet they shot that guy in our kitchen."

"But—" Daphna said, seeing the obvious now. She turned around to face the Secret Keeper now. *"Why?"* she demanded. "You've been trying to *kill* us."

"Priorities have changed," the Secret Keeper said. "I can assure you that we are no longer seeking your deaths. On the contrary."

"What if we start telling everyone about our ribs," Dex challenged. He had no idea why. "What if we tell the whole world that Jesus' mother had one, and so did he, and that's how he was born *and* how he came back from the dead? Because we figured that out, too."

"Dexter—" Daphna warned.

"By all means," was the Secret Keeper surprising response. "Please let me know how we might help facilitate whatever it is you see fit to do."

"Because now we're friends," Daphna sneered.

"We are not friends," the old man assured the twins. "Of that you can be absolutely certain. Quite the opposite. We have simply figured out who you really are."

"And who is that?" the twins both asked.

"For his arrogance, for his pride, for his refusal to serve man," the Secret Keeper recited, "the great Dragon was thrown down not long after the Creation of the world, the Serpent of old who is called the Devil and Satan, who deceives the whole world: he was thrown down to the Earth, and—"

"Not to Earth," Daphna corrected. "He was locked inside a book in Heaven, his *Book,* I guess."

"You are the Lawless One. You are the Man of

Sin."

"What?" Dex said. "Which one of us? Me?"

"The fact that there are two of you is what delayed our apprehension of the truth. One of you is it. Which one, matters not."

"Look," Dex said, growing tired of this. "Why don't you just tell us what you're talking about. Otherwise, thanks for your generous offer to help, but we're in kind of a hurry."

"And then that Lawless One," the Secret Keeper continued, quoting whatever it was he was quoting, "will be revealed whom the Lord will slay with the breath of His mouth and bring to an end by the appearance of His coming; that is, the one whose coming is in accord with the activity of Satan, with all power and signs and false wonders, and with all the deception of wickedness—"

"Right, then," Dex said. "Let's go, Daphna." He put his hand on the door latch.

"Wait," Daphna said. "This sounds familiar. I read about this stuff. He's talking about the second coming of Jesus, about what they call the End of Times. There are all these signs like wars and earthquakes and—*plagues.*" Daphna could not help but pause a moment as the contents of this list reverberated in her mind. She could see it doing the same in her brother's. "It's all brought on," she continued, forcing it aside, "by the appearance of—*Wait a minute!*"

"I write to you," the Secret Keeper went on, "not because you do not know the truth, but because you know it, and know that no lie is of the truth. Who is the liar but he who denies that Jesus is the Christ? This is the Antichrist."

"*Um,*" Dex said, trying to sort through all the mumbo jumbo. "Is he calling one of us the *Antichrist?*"

The Secret Keeper just sat there now in the half-wrecked Hummer with his hideous hair and stared at the twins as this washed over them.

"Why would you help us if you think—?" Dex started to ask, but Daphna interrupted him with the answer.

"Because they believe that when the Antichrist comes, so does Satan, and then the Apocalypse—the end of the world. And with *that*, Jesus will return. They want us to make that all happen."

"As I said," the Secret Keeper told the twins, "let me know how we can help."

CHAPTER SEVENTEEN
The Book of Blood

"Guard Quinn," Daphna demanded.

The Secret Keeper nodded. "Of course," he said, "but I'm offering much more substantial assistance. I'm offering to help you find the Holy Grail."

"You know where it is?" This was, once again, both twins.

"We believe it is precisely where most people think it is," the Secret Keeper told them, "in King Solomon's Temple, in the Holy of Holies, which is in the Well of Souls. Are you familiar with this sacred chamber?"

"Of course we are," Daphna snapped, looking at her brother. They both knew at once this had to be the well Daphna heard Mr. Brown and his group of angels argue about—the well Mr. Brown thought they could never search without getting killed. "If you know it's there," she challenged anyway, "why don't you find it yourself? The Temple couldn't have been that large."

"The Temple was 90 feet long, 20 feet wide, and 45 feet high," the Secret Keeper informed her. "The Holy of Holies was in the innermost sanctuary, shrouded in total darkness. Only the High Priest could enter it. Anyone else would be struck instantly dead."

The twins looked at each other. Mr. G didn't tell them this.

"Inside was kept the Arc of the Covenant," the Secret Keeper continued, "which contained the tablets of the Ten Commandments, along with other sacred objects."

"Like the *Book of*—" Dex started to say, but Daphna, on instinct, jabbed him in the side.

"Indeed, like the Book of Blood."

"The *what?*" two voices cried.

"You are surprised. Perhaps you do not know all you think you know." Then the Secret Keeper enlightened his new pupils: "Joseph of Arimathea," he explained, "stood by the cross with a book to take down Jesus' last words. Instead, he captured the blood of our Savior on its pages."

The twins took this in a moment, then Daphna said, "We saw that picture at the Vatican, someone catching his blood in—the actual Grail, I guess it's supposed to be. But now that I think about it, why would he be standing there with a golden cup?"

"That plaque in the Vatican," Dex said, "with the tapestry of the Last Supper. Jesus was saying, 'This cup is the new testament in my blood.' We already know he was talking about a book."

"Right!"

Neither twin saw any reason to mention Mr. G's theory that the Grail was the Book of Letters, so neither did. Because it didn't matter what it was—as long as it got them the Book of the Living back, and the means to add names to it.

"The problem," the Secret Keeper continued, "is that the remains of the Temple are underneath the Temple Mount in Jerusalem, possibly under the Dome of the Rock or the El Aksa Mosque. Mostly likely it is somewhere between the two. These are Muslim holy places. Archaeological studies have been forbidden there. To defile any of the land would be an act of war—Holy war."

"Then why are you offering to help us defile it?" Daphna asked.

"Because a holy war is probably a good start if you're aiming for the Apocalypse," Dex said. "And there's chaos there right now. Fighting. You saw it on the news. So the timing is perfect. But what I don't get is what's so great about a book with Jesus' blood on its pages?"

"DNA," Daphna guessed, though she knew she was right. "You want to clone him, don't you?" she asked the awful man with his awful hair. "You want to bring Jesus back yourself. I'll bet you haven't risked going for the book before because the technology wasn't ready. But now it's close enough, and you're running out of time."

"Despite the deteriorating situation," the Secret Keeper replied, getting down to business, "the Temple Mount will be protected at all costs, by many parties. Even so, there has never been a better opportunity than that which we are presented with at this moment in history. The stars, as they say, are aligning. You must travel there swiftly and gain entry into the underground chambers. There are ways."

"Let's just say we were willing to help you," Daphna said, "which we aren't. How are we supposed to get there when no one is allowed to fly, and even if we did get there, how are we supposed to find it? And if we did find it, how are we supposed to get it without being struck instantly dead?"

"It is a measure of the enormity of this crisis," the Secret Keeper said, "that despite her immense influence, even the Church has thus far been unable to find a way around the flight ban—though we are working on it. But I have no doubt you will find a way to obtain the Book should you decide to do so. I can tell you one more thing that perhaps might be of assistance. We know of a fragment believed to have been written by Joseph of Arimathea, who was charged by Jesus, before he died, to hide and protect the *Book of Blood*. Some believe that Joseph and a group of followers he gathered, a group eventually identified as the Knights Templar, spirited it off to England, and that they have protected it ever since."

"So that's why most of the Grail stories are set there," Daphna said. "King Arthur and all that." She couldn't help it. The knowledge thrilled her.

"It is our understanding," the Secret Keeper continued, unimpressed, "that the stories were meant to distract those who might search for the book. We believe Joseph hid it in the Temple *before* traveling, that his circuitous journey was meant to suggest many possible hiding spots."

"What's on this fragment?" Dex asked.

"Quite simply that the 'Grail,' as he chose to call it, was 'set in stone in King Solomon's Temple.'"

"I guess that's something," Daphna said.

"It is possible," the Secret Keeper added, "that the sentence itself reveals the hiding place."

"A code?" Dex asked. They did codes. Sort of.

"A cipher of some sort, no doubt."

"Do the Hebrew words have other meanings?" Daphna asked. "Have you tried to figure out their numerical values?"

"Joseph, like Jesus," the Secret Keeper explained,

"probably spoke Aramaic, but also like Jesus probably knew Hebrew and Greek. He was well educated, so it's not unlikely that he knew some English as well. And as it turns out," he added, "the fragment was written, we understand, in English."

"Because he was in England?"

"Very likely."

Daphna processed all this for a moment. It wasn't much to go on. *Set in stone?* "Anyway," she said, snapping out of it, "if you think we're going to traipse halfway around the world and find the Holy Grail, then turn around and hand it over to you, you've got another thing—"

"We want you to do with it exactly what you are no doubt planning to do."

"And what's that?"

"Deliver it to Satan, of course, so that he may bring down Armageddon."

The twins just looked at the Secret Keeper's droopy eyes for a long moment. Then they looked at each other.

"Wait a minute," Daphna said one more time. "None of this makes sense. You were trying to kill us so we wouldn't tell the world the truth about Jesus' Virgin Birth. That means he's *not* the savior any more than we are. So why would he be coming back? It's not logical."

"And how are you supposed to clone Jesus, anyway," Dex added, "if we give the book with his blood in it to the Devil?"

The Secret Keeper merely shook his head at the twins like a disappointed teacher. "The circumstances of our savior's birth, death, and resurrection are not important," he said, "except to those who require fantastic stories to believe. We do not know exactly how Satan will spur his return. Nor do we know how the Book of Blood will find its way into our hands. We do not require such knowledge because we have scripture, and we have something else as well, something you don't know the slightest thing about."

"And what would that be?" Dexter asked.

"Faith."

The twins had no response to this, so they said nothing.

"By the way," the Secret Keeper added, apparently finished with his lesson, "who is the unconscious girl in the back?"

CHAPTER EIGHTEEN
Tickets

The Secret Keeper nodded, so the men in black allowed the wide-eyed twins to climb down out of the Hummer. They ran around to the back, which was brutally gouged and dented. Dex wrestled with the bent latch until it cooperated, and the door rose up to reveal Branwen lying there in a filthy, forlorn heap, battered, bruised, and unconscious.

"She must have followed us to Dr. Fludd's from Mr. G's," Dex guessed, "and she must have gotten into the garage after that car broke it in. She probably hit her head bouncing around back here."

Despite having spared Branwen a few compassionate thoughts last night, Daphna now couldn't find an ounce of sympathy for the girl. In fact, she had pounds of—what was the word? There was a German word for enjoying the suffering of others. If anyone deserved this comedown, it was Branwen. What was she doing stalking them like some psycho killer in a horror film?

"We need to get her in to the doctor," Dex said, watching the Secret Keeper watch him back. "Dr. Lewis, right?"

"What?" Daphna asked. "You're kidding, right?"

"We should at least let him have a look at her."

"What do you care? *Wait,*" Daphna said, cutting her eyes, "don't tell me you want to help her just because she's so—"

"No!" Dex protested. "It's just—It doesn't seem—"

"She's trying to *kill* us," Daphna pointed out. "Or me, anyway. Just leave her here. In fact, we'd be wise just to roll the truck into some heavy traffic and—"

"I'm just saying that it doesn't seem—righteous."

"Oh, all right!" Daphna conceded, exasperated. She didn't want to waste any more time arguing or trying to understand her brother's irrational whims.

It was because Branwen was so beautiful, she was sure of it. She looked good even now, when she was a complete and total disaster. *"C'mon,"* Daphna sighed. "But I guarantee we'll regret it."

The twins worked together to get Branwen out of the truck. Fortunately, like all Pops, she weighed virtually nothing. They draped her arms over their shoulders and got her to her feet, her toes anyway. Daphna carried the library book about communicating with angels in her free hand.

The men in black made sure there were no problems on the street. They were everywhere, it seemed, sealing off the entire area, aiming guns in all directions. They seemed utterly unaffected by the heat, which, though steadily diminishing, still made the twins want to keel over.

Ignoring the Masons on the ground around the Hummer, the twins walked, or dragged, Branwen through the now broken-out entryway of the wellness center.

As Dex was looking at the various doors around the circular interior of the place, Daphna suddenly let go of Branwen. "Can you handle her?" she asked, making Dex scramble to avoid dropping her. Without waiting for his answer, she took off, sprinting toward the opposite side of the center. Once she reached the far end, she burst through an unmarked door.

Dex shook his head and went about hauling the stupid skinny Pop along as quickly as he could, regretting the decision to help her. However insubstantial she was, it was difficult and awkward getting her moving by himself. He finally reached the door and managed to work the knob, but not without extreme irritation. He did that throat-breathing thing, then pushed the door open with his foot.

Initially, Dexter thought it was just an office, because his first glimpse inside was of a giant desk and couch, but when the door swung all the way open he saw it was an actual operating room. Quinn was lying on a silver table under blue blankets, hooked up to all kinds of machines and tubes. Machines were all around him, including one that looked like a chest freezer attached to a laundry machine. Most of the machines had cords running in an unwieldy tangle to another machine sitting under the operating table—

the auxiliary power source.

Daphna had Quinn's hand. She was blubbering about how sorry she was. An old man in a lab coat with mad scientist hair was trying to get her away. Dr. Lewis, Dex assumed. The guy was slight and rather feeble, but looked super smart with that hair, anyway.

"Careful!" the doctor cried in a high, almost girlish, voice. He was tugging weakly at Daphna's shirt. "Careful!"

"Is he okay?" Daphna asked, reluctantly letting go of Quinn's hand.

"He is stable," Dr. Lewis told her, "but I don't hope for a quick return at this point." Then he said, "Now, we must act quickly if you are to go."

"Go?" Daphna said. "Where?"

"To Purgatory!" Dr. Lewis seemed surprised by the question. "I think I understand what went wrong with the boy. I—"

"No!" Daphna snapped, incensed. "Absolutely not! We're not doing that operation! We know there's no such thing as Purgatory, and we know you were trying kill Quinn's soul!"

This definitely surprised the doctor. "How—?"

"It's what we do," Dex said.

At the sound of his voice, Daphna and Dr. Lewis turned to find Dexter standing in the door with Branwen barely in his grasp.

"What is this?" the doctor demanded.

"Ah, little help?"

"We think she hit her head," Daphna said as she helped Dex maneuver Branwen to the couch. "Can you take a quick look?" Then they could get rid of her.

"We have no time for this," Dr. Lewis warned. But then he said, "Wait a moment." He approached the couch and leaned down to lift Branwen's eyelids for a moment. "She may have brain trauma," he conjectured, looking back at the twins. "We will send *her* to the Realm of Dead Souls!"

Just then Branwen gave out a moan. Her eyes fluttered a bit. *"Teal?"* she whined. *"Wren?"*

Dr. Lewis examined her further, lifting up her eyelids again and feeling her neck and skull. "It may be just a concussion," he decided. "We'll have to see if she comes out of it. Now," he added, clearly leaving the subject of Branwen behind, "if Mr. Brown sent you back, then he must—"

"Mr. Brown is dead," Dex said.

"Impossible."

"And anyway," Daphna said, ignoring the look of horror on the doctor's face, "the book is not in the Realm of Dead Souls. It's in Jerusalem—in the Well of Souls."

"But he cannot be—!"

"And it doesn't matter that storming it would be suicide for the Colors," Dex said. "Because they're all dead."

This was too much. Dr. Lewis staggered backward a few steps.

"We were told by the man who knows even more than the Pope that the Well is under the ancient temple in Jerusalem, but that the remains are not accessible," Dex explained, "because they're under a holy site."

Dr. Lewis did not respond to this. He was running a hand through his crazy hair, thinking hard.

"And he said the book has Jesus' blood in it," Daphna told him anyway, "not the Secret Name."

To this Dr. Lewis also did not reply. His eyes were darting around the room while he continued to rake his hair.

Dex turned to Daphna and asked, "Why would all the angels in Heaven be searching for a book with a Lamed Vavnik's blood in it? And how would it ever have been in Heaven for Jesus to steal if Joseph Whoever caught his blood in it when he was dying? None of it makes sense. The Secret Keeper is either lying— and he's always lying—or he's totally wrong about the book."

Daphna had no reaction to these seemingly valid points. It would be beyond stupid not to assume they were being used. The question was exactly how, and by whom? She approached Quinn on the operating table, took his hand again, closed her eyes, and started feather breathing.

"Daphna—" Dex said.

"I need to talk to him," she said through gritted teeth. "I need to know if he thinks the Secret Keeper is telling the truth, at least about where the book is."

"I think it's safe to say—"

"He *is* probably lying," Daphna admitted, looking at Dex again. "He probably wants to send us on a wild goose chase, to get us far away for some reason. And it doesn't really matter what's in the book if we never find it! *How are we supposed to get to Jerusalem, anyway?* I want to know what Quinn thinks. You should try with Nora."

"*Teal—Wren,*" Branwen muttered.

"We need to made contact, Dex," Daphna pressed. "We need to make it *now.*"

"Isn't that why we got that library book?"

Daphna looked down at the book she'd unconsciously set on the edge of the operating table. She'd forgotten all about it. Without further comment, she hurried over to the chair behind the giant desk in the back of the room, sat down, and started flipping pages.

The wild-haired doctor was still standing there looking totally mental and Daphna was already lost in the book, so Dex scanned the room. It was like some kind of science fiction laboratory with all the pumps and dials and beeping lights. For some reason there were gumdrops stuck to toothpicks in a crunched-up pile on the floor.

He realized he was thirsty, incredibly thirsty.

Dex approached the long machine that looked like a refrigerator chest. "Any chance this thing is full of sodas?" he asked, running his finger over the buttons on top.

"Stop!" Lewis cried, snapping out of his trance. He reached out to Dex with twitching fingers, as if to stop him by magic. "Do not touch that!" he ordered. "It's a Cryogenic freezer! For body parts—organs!"

"Ah," Dex said, stepping back. 'Organs' was not a word he wanted to think about ever again. "In that case," he said, "maybe I'll take a pass on the refreshments."

"*Teal!*" Branwen moaned. "*Wrennnn!*"

"'Angels are celestial beings who carry out the will of God,'" Daphna announced after looking up from her book, then over at Wren, who was clearly not all there yet. If she woke up they'd best be ready to deal with her. "'References to them can be found in the Old and New Testaments,'" she read, looking down again, "'as well as many other religious traditions—' I'm reading the intro," she explained. Then she flipped a page and went back to furiously skimming.

"Did you know you were working for angels?" Dex asked Dr. Lewis.

"Yes, of course! I was their doctor!"

"'Angel-like beings,'" Daphna read, "'can be traced back to Sumer, the world's first civilization.'"

"Angels get sick?" Dex asked the doctor.

"They have—medical needs."

"'In Egyptian symbolism, wings equal divine protection.'"

"I don't see how they could have hidden those wings," Dex said.

To this, Dr. Lewis did not reply.

"'Angels are in constant conflict with the forces of Satan.'"

"They'd have to wear gigantic backpacks or something to hide them. There's no way they fold flat, not wings that huge. Could they?"

Dr. Lewis again declined to answer.

"'Swedenborg states that people are born to become angels.'" Daphna was seizing on whatever jumped off the pages, but there just wasn't time for a thorough investigation.

"Maybe they shrink when they aren't needed," Dex conjectured. "That would be freaky."

"'Jewish mystics speak of humans becoming angels.' Humans *becoming* angels," Daphna repeated, looking up. "I wonder if they mean it's possible while they're still alive—"

"If the wings grew and shrank, why didn't they use them to get away from the Masons?" Dex asked. "Running up the walls wasn't enough. They could have just flown up to the ceiling."

"'Hermes sped through the world on winged sandals.'"

"That'd be nice," Dex said, looking over at Daphna, "flying shoes." Then he looked at Dr. Lewis one more time and said, "What are they, Velcro?"

The doctor looked at Dexter, just for a moment. It was an involuntary glance, and Dex did not miss the fear that flashed in his eyes.

"Dex," Daphna said, seeing the expression forming on her brother's face. "What is it?"

"He said they have 'medical needs.'"

"So?"

"When the angels left Heaven—" Dex said. His face began to flush as he realized what it was he was realizing. "They were stuck here forever, right? How could they go around looking for the Book of Letters with gigantic wings on their backs? Might be a little conspicuous don't you think? They had to live among men. Which meant—"

"They had to look like men!" Daphna leapt to her feet.

"Mr. Brown told me you weren't normal children," said Dr. Lewis. "Yes. There—" he added, pointing.

At the freezer.

The twins rushed to it.

"If the Church is correct and the Book is indeed in the Well of Souls," Dr. Lewis told them. "I can help you get there."

Dex and Daphna turned back to the doctor.

"You believe them? After all this stuff about the Realm?"

"The Realm of Dead Souls is not secret to the Church. And while they may lack the knowledge I have about accessing it, the fact that they are not trying to, but are rather seeking entry into the Well—this is very persuasive." He nodded at the chest. "Open the latches."

There were two large latches on either side of the lid.

"But one moment!" Dr. Lewis cried before either of the twins moved to open it. He went to the taller machine attached to the freezer and pressed some of the red and green buttons on its face. There were beeps and hisses.

Then he nodded.

The twins freed the latches, then lifted the lid. They stepped back at the sound of a motor coming to life. Vapor of some sort rose out of the chest, so nothing inside was visible at first.

But it cleared quickly, and the twins could see compartments being raised. When they were up, they found themselves looking at four long, frozen white bundles—four sets of wings, six-foot long, ivory-feathered wings, wrapped round themselves.

The vapor poured off of them, making them

seem to steam.

"For thousands of years they retained their wings," Dr. Lewis explained. "They moved about only in darkness and shadow. Eventually one of them Severed and let his wings die. When he himself did not die, another Severed. And she found the wings could be preserved with trace amounts of nitrogen, though barely."

"Nitrogen?"

"Eventually, luckily, before any others tried, they found me."

"Was Mr. Brown the first one to sever with you?" Dex asked.

Lewis nodded.

"What's happening?" Daphna asked. The vapor was pouring off the wings much more rapidly now and in greater volume.

"They are not like human tissue," Dr. Lewis explained. "They are defrosting. It takes only a few moments."

"They—they—you—" Daphna stuttered as the implication of what she was seeing and hearing dawned on her. She hadn't let it sink in. "You *amputated their wings?*"

"But they go back on," Dex said. "And guess what."

"What?"

"We just got our tickets to Jerusalem."

CHAPTER NINETEEN
Joining

With Quinn on the operating table and Branwen on the couch, the desk was their only option. After clearing it, Dr. Lewis had the twins lay face down, shoulder to shoulder, with their feet hanging over the edge. They'd nearly come to blows over who would undergo what Dr. Lewis called "Joining" first, but the issue was settled when he said they could do it together.

Dr. Lewis leaned over Daphna with a pair of surgical scissors and cut a long slit in the back of her T-shirt, from just below her collar to just above the bottom seam. Then he did the same to Dexter's.

"I must warn you," he said. "When Mr. Brown Rejoined, it was somewhat—uncomfortable. And for him they were natural. The muscles will attach themselves to your arteries and veins. It's really quite extraordinary. I could give you something for the pain first, but I'd worry whether that might hinder your bodies' willingness to accept the—"

"Don't worry about it," Daphna said. "We don't have time to waste recovering, anyway." But she was terrified. Pain was not her forte.

"Are you're sure we'll be able to fly halfway around the world with those things?" Dex asked.

"Absolutely," Dr. Lewis promised. "These are not the wings of birds you are Joining."

"All right then," Dex said. "Let's just get this over with."

"Brace yourselves. This won't take long."

The twins looked at each other, then up at a mirror that showed Dr. Lewis behind them carefully lifting a set of wings out of its compartment. He grasped it tightly with both hands, as if it might fly away on its own, then let it unfurl. Dex and Daphna's eyes went wide. The wings were covered with shining alabaster feathers as long as their arms.

Dr. Lewis had the tips of each great wing in his grasp now, and he was walking the set carefully over to the desk. They swelled in his hands, as if a heart were beating inside them.

The twins gasped.

Hanging freely where they met were what looked like the ends of exposed nerves, and they were twitching.

"Oh, God," Daphna said as the doctor laid one of the heavy bundles on her exposed back. She was having serious second thoughts. But raising her eyes to the mirror again, she saw Quinn lying there inert. She closed her eyes and clenched her teeth. The wings pressed her down into the desktop, but otherwise she felt nothing.

Dr. Lewis went back for the second bundle and set it on Dexter's back. "Wow," Dexter said, "they weigh a ton." But it didn't hurt. Not at all.

"It's tickling!" Daphna laughed. It felt like sharp fingernails were gently raking the skin on either side of her spine.

Dex looked at her and began to roll his eyes, but suddenly he was laughing, too.

But now Daphna cried out, choking on her laughter. It felt as if those nails were digging into her skin now. Dex grunted as he felt the same thing.

"Ow!" Daphna cried. "Oww!" The digging was now a stabbing, piercing pain. Dex felt it. He grunted harder, clenching his teeth.

"Hold on," Doctor Lewis urged. "It's only just beginning."

"Teal?" Branwen called out from the couch. "Wren? Where are you?"

The doctor wasn't exaggerating. The twins' pain intensified by the second, until they were both crying out, both gripping the edge of the desk, squeezing it with white knuckles.

Daphna tried to take feather breaths, pulling them one after another deep into her belly, holding them in for the briefest time she could. In through her nose, out through her mouth. In through her nose, out through her mouth. A perfect circle. Dex saw this and tried his throat breathing, taking in as much oxygen as he possibly could. Nora! he thought.

But it was useless.

The pain doubled, tripled. Then it doubled and tripled again. Needles were not only stabbing them now, but burrowing into their flesh, triggering riptides of pain through the nerves in their back and under their arms.

Daphna wailed. She rolled on to her side to see her brother, but the agony was blinding. All she could do was reach for him.

Dex reached back, and the twins clutched each other's hands, screaming their lungs out, forgetting everything but the pain and each other.

In wasn't long before they forgot even each other.

And then, finally, mercifully, they forgot themselves, too.

CHAPTER TWENTY
Hybrids

Daphna heard squeaking: wheels on a hard floor. She opened her eyes.

Instead of seeing the floor beyond the edge of the desk, she was seeing the operating room's textured white ceiling. "Dex?" she ventured, confused and afraid. But she sensed him there, next to her.

Dex opened his eyes and blinked, baffled and bleary as well. He was also on his back.

Daphna felt no pain, but she couldn't move. Nothing seemed to be restraining her, which meant—she was paralyzed. "Why can't I move?" she demanded. "Did something go wrong?"

"It's temporary," said Dr. Lewis from somewhere she couldn't see. There was that squeaking again, and then his face loomed upside down over hers. He'd been pushing one of those large machines over to the desk. Its wheels needed oil.

"What happened?" Dex asked. Dr. Lewis had a bloodstained bandage wrapped around his head, mashing down a portion of his crazy hair.

"What time is it?" Daphna asked. "Tell me why I can't move!"

"It's morning," Dr. Lewis said. "You passed out from the pain."

"Morning? It's tomorrow! Dex! We have eight days now!"

"Do not despair," said Dr. Lewis. "If all goes well, we shall solve all our problems today. Now, in fact."

"Did the wings not—take?" Daphna asked. Now that she thought about it, there was some slight tingling in her back, but she couldn't tell whether anything was attached. "What happened to your head?"

"The girl," Dr. Lewis said. "She attacked me. I Joined her after you passed out, thinking a test would be prudent. She surely passed out, too, but where I couldn't—"

"You gave Branwen wings?" Daphna wailed. She tried to turn her head to Dex, but she wasn't able.

"To successfully send a subject to the Realm, I have determined that a Hybrid is required."

"But—!" Daphna objected, but then remembered having heard the word 'hybrid' before, though she couldn't remember when or where. But then she did. And then she suddenly understood a great many things. "Dex," she said, "I know why Mr. Brown kept Mr. G away from the Colors, why he never told him what they were doing."

"Why?"

"It was Mr. Brown's theory that the Grail is in the Realm of Dead Souls. The others were not convinced. One of them said it didn't matter anyway, because they didn't have a Hybrid to try it out on—I had no idea what that meant and forgot all about it, but 'it' had to be the Standstill operation, and a 'Hybrid' has to be someone part human and part angel. You could kill the part that's angel to send it to the Realm of Dead Souls, but bring the rest of it back—the part that's human."

"But he did have someone," Dex said, "his son."

"Mr. Brown had a son?" Dr. Lewis cried.

"He was protecting him," Daphna explained. "Don't you see? He didn't want to risk his own son, not even to find the Holy Grail. Poor Mr. G!"

There was a moment of silence while the twins let this settle over them. Then the obvious dawned.

"No!" Daphna shrieked. "You're not doing it to us! You said you believed it was in the Well of Souls! LIAR!" She tried to force her body to move, but it was dead weight. "Help!" she screamed at the ceiling. "Help! *Help!*"

Dr. Lewis did not seem alarmed by Daphna's cries. On the contrary, he began calmly laying out various surgical instruments onto a rolling cart he'd also wheeled over. "I do believe them," he said.

"HELP!" Daphna roared. *"HEL*—What?"

Dr. Lewis was washing his hands now. "I have no interest in these forbidden books," he explained. "For power is not what I seek. I've known for a long time that Heaven exists. Now I want to know if the same can be said of the Realm of Dead Souls. What I seek is knowledge, and true knowledge requires irrefutable proof. It took many years to convince Brown that the Book was there rather than the Well, where of course it must be."

Daphna didn't know what to say to this, and that made her realize that Dexter hadn't said anything in quite a while. She turned her head to see why.

"You turned your head," he whispered when she looked at him.

Daphna looked back up at the ceiling, hoping Dr. Lewis hadn't seen.

"I can feel them," Dex whispered.

A moment later Dr. Lewis appeared over Dexter with a syringe.

Dex sat up and took it from him.

"Too quickly!" the doctor yelped, backing away. "Too quickly! Your ribs! I did not account for your ribs!"

Daphna sat up too. She felt—wonderful. She and Dex got up off the desk.

Brother and sister beheld each other.

They had wings.

CHAPTER TWENTY-ONE
Abomination

"I can *move* them," Daphna said, nearly speechless. Her wings opened and closed behind her. "Dex," she spluttered, "they're—they're *mine*. It's no different from moving my arm." She moved her arm as if to prove her point. Her arm felt strong. Really strong.

Dexter moved his wings while looking up over his shoulder in disbelief. Daphna was right. They were every bit a part of him as any other part. *He. Had. Wings.*

Dr. Lewis cowered among his machines.

"Take care of Quinn," Daphna ordered him. "Take care of him or else."

"I will kill him!" Dr. Lewis snarled. "I will kill him if one of you does not let me—!"

"Is there a problem here?" someone asked, someone who'd come into the room. "Good Lord!"

The twins turned to see the Secret Keeper with two of his men in black. They were all staring, agog, at the twins.

"It's about time," Dex complained.

"Make him take care of Quinn," Daphna demanded. "That's what you said you'd do! That's what will help us do—what we're doing."

The Secret Keeper's eyes were riveted by her wings, but he nodded. "It will be done," he promised.

"Good," said Daphna. "Now, you'll have to excuse us. We're going to Jerusalem. And all I have to say is, the book better be there."

Daphna retrieved her library book from the drawer she'd put it in before the Joining and tucked it between some feathers under one of her wings. Then she walked over and kissed Quinn on the lips. After that, with her head held Branwen-high, she walked out of the room. Dex followed her, but not before pausing in front of the Secret Keeper. He looked the baggy-faced, curtain-haired old fart in the eye and said, "How do you like me now?"

"An abomination," was all the Secret Keeper had to say.

Dex swallowed into a suddenly dry throat, unable to produce a reply. He felt quite certain that he could leap on the old man and break him to pieces with his bare hands. Instead, he headed out into the wellness center after his sister.

Daphna was sprinting through it again, so he ran after her.

He saw her hit the sidewalk outside, then—

She was in the air.

But only for a second. Almost immediately, she spun completely onto her back, then fell like a sack of potatoes on the sidewalk. But just as suddenly she was up again, leaping into the air. This time she got some height, rising right up over the Secret Keeper's SUV, but her shoe clipped its roof, and then she was tumbling head over heels onto the street.

When he reached the SUV, Dex saw that his sister's foot had dented its roof. He found her lying behind it on the pavement, grinning—beaming and grinning. The men in black, still stationed around the street and on top of the buildings all around, stared at them with fear and fascination. Every one of them crossed himself.

"Try it," is all Daphna said, getting to her feet. Despite her first two attempts having utterly failed, she'd never felt so exhilarated.

"How?" Dex asked, but even as he asked, he was willing himself into the air. It was a combination of simply standing up so straight that your head wants to lift right off your neck and flapping your wings. Just like that, he was airborne—but then, like his sister, he immediately and involuntarily twisted round, then fell in a heap.

"I guess it takes a time or two," Daphna said.

Dex was back up, now hurtling through the air, spinning like a top.

Then he was slamming into the building across the street and crashing to the pavement in a shower of bricks and dust. He'd broken his fall with his wings and wasn't hurt at all. The wings were strong, incredibly strong. All of him was. Dex picked up a hunk of brick he's smashed out of the wall and crushed it to powder in his hand.

Daphna rushed over to find her brother smiling ear-to-ear. "See?" she said.

"It's incredible!"

The twins saw that the Secret Keeper had come back outside to watch them.

"How's this for abomination!" Dex yelled.

He burst into the sky again. And this time he did not fall. Dex twisted as he rose, but less. He already understood the need to flap with equal force on each side. Dex rose with speed and power, pumping his tremendous wings.

Daphna stared at her brother admiringly for a moment, then burst into the air herself. It was already easier for her, too. Much easier. She flew behind Dexter, who was now making large, wide circles over the wellness center. It sounded like he was screaming, which alarmed her, but when she got close enough, she found he was simply letting loose with pure, primal, joy. He shot away, soaring into the distance over Portland, so Daphna took off after him, letting loose her own soul-cleansing scream. She cut her own path through the hot air, pumping and screaming and just simply—flying.

CHAPTER TWENTY-TWO
The Heart of the Plume

Dexter had no idea where he was going, and he didn't care. His eyes weren't even open. He was just going, flapping his prodigious wings with propulsive, muscular strokes. He stretched his arms out like Superman.

He *was* Superman.

But Dex sensed something wasn't right and opened his eyes. Daphna was nowhere in sight. The shock of this realization made him stop flapping his wings, which made him start to fall. But after a terrifying few moments, he recovered, finding he could simply hover with gentle wing strokes.

There she was, way above him, flying straight up toward the clouds.

"Daphna!" Dex shouted. "Daphna! Forget it! You're not going to find a Gate!"

She didn't respond, so Dex sped toward her. She was fast, but he was faster. He gained on her quickly.

As Daphna flew, making a beeline for the vault of the sky, she scanned the horizon. Gates were here, somewhere, maybe everywhere. *One* had to be, anyway. Maybe they were visible to the human eye if you knew what you were looking for, if you could recognize the telltale shimmering seams she and Dex had seen so clearly in the Aleph. Or maybe they'd be visible to angel eyes. Daphna could tell her eyes, like the rest of her, were much stronger. She felt like she could see for miles.

Quinn, she thought. *I'm coming to get you.*

Daphna flew right up into and out of a cloud—a burst of white that wet her face. She hardly noticed it.

Where? she thought. *Where!*

Daphna suddenly stopped, gasping. She was too high, and now she couldn't breathe. Panic gripped her as she began to fall out of the sky, but suddenly her brother was there, holding her up.

"Hover!" he shouted, letting them slowly lose altitude.

Daphna was breathing again, and she was able to start flapping her wings just enough to hold steady. Her lungs were extra-strong, but they were a human's extra-strong lungs, and they needed air. Dex let go of her.

"I've got to reach him!"

"Look," Dex said, pointing down into the distance.

There, rising in a massive plume, was a cloud of black and mustard-colored smoke. Dex sensed that his eyes were like a hawk's—*better than a hawk's*—so he could tell it was Gabriel Park, what *used* to be Gabriel Park.

"Oh, my God," Daphna said. "That's the park." She took off toward it.

Dex rushed up alongside her.

"Careful," Daphna said, pulling up before they got too close. There were planes circling the foul cloud, military planes.

"It stinks!" Dex pulled his shirt up over his nose.

The plume smelled like nothing they'd ever smelled before. No, that wasn't true. It was like the stench of the abyss they'd fallen into outside of Eden. But even worse.

It was as they'd seen on TV: the park was simply gone, and in its place was a gargantuan hole, fuming and frothing with that pestilential smoke.

The hole was surrounded by what couldn't be less than five hundred army vehicles, police cars, fire trucks, and ambulances. A cordon of soldiers was set up around the rim, though no one, it seemed, was interested in getting too close to it. The twins looked around in other directions. The streets, for the most part, were quiet.

"Hellmouth," Daphna said, looking back at the hole with her shirt up over her nose as well.

A terrific, whirring noise made the twins look up to their left, where a compact armored helicopter had appeared. They prepared to rush off, but it took no notice of them. It was heading, slowly, into the heart of the plume.

"I think it's some kind of cave explorer," Dex said. The thing had all kinds of winches and cables coiled up on it.

The helicopter, highly maneuverable, was now hovering just over the hole, fully enveloped now by the thicker, darker smoke it was drawing up out of the depths. Powerful lights pointing down from underneath it came on, lighting up the smoke in an eerie, otherworldly way.

Slowly, carefully, the craft began to descend.

"Ah," said Dex, unconsciously drifting away from the scene. "I'm thinking this is probably not a good idea."

Daphna backed off alongside her brother, holding her breath.

A moment later, the moment before the copter dipped out of sight completely, a burst of black fire shot out of the hole. The flaming Dragon head took shape for just an instant—impossible, colossal—and it swallowed the craft.

But the head vanished as quickly as it appeared. The copter was still there, but out of control, its pilot panicking. The craft listed badly to the side, and the propellers clipped the rim of the pit. There was the sound of tearing metal, and then the helicopter fell into the smoke.

After a long, terrifying silence, there was an explosion below. Flames burst up through the plume, which was, just then, swept aside by a powerful gust of wind.

Now panic erupted among the personnel on the ground.

"Look!" Daphna cried. There was a narrow ledge winding around the pit walls, circling down into darkness below.

But smoke was filling the pit again. Moments later it was spilling out of the crater as it had before.

"Which way is Israel?" Dexter asked.

"What?"

"Which way is Jerusalem?"

It took a moment for Daphna to process the question. "East," she said when she finally did. She pointed in the general direction. "But it's a fifteen-hour plane trip, at least. You don't *really* think we could—"

Dex shot away, pumping his wings, flying east.

Daphna took a long, deep breath down into her belly, feathered it, then slowly let it out. When the time was right she was going to let him have it about this.

About Branwen too. After one more feather breath, she flew off after him.

CHAPTER TWENTY-THREE
Winging It

The twins didn't speak as they flew. They made no plan other than just to fly. So they flew. What they saw left them speechless, anyway.

The Waterfront was a shambles: Most of the docks had been somehow smashed, motorboats floated upside down around the Willamette like bath toys, and forsaken cars and trucks lined the bridges—all the bridges.

Helicopters were pretty much everywhere. It seemed like the only way the authorities could get around. Perhaps that was why the Martial Law seemed less than entirely effective. For the most part, the streets were quiet, but there were roving gangs here and there breaking into buildings.

Looking for books.

The twins flew on, passing over Northeast Portland. It looked much the same. Ditched vehicles, broken windows, burning houses. They saw a library being looted.

"It's not there!" Dex shouted. Did those idiots really think giving the Holy Grail to the *Devil* would earn them a reward?

Do you? he asked himself.

Dex wondered just how many people were willing to do such a thing—sell out the world to save their own skin. If what he and Daphna had seen on the news was accurate, the answer was a lot. Dex didn't doubt that almost everyone would be out doing the same thing if they weren't at home, hiding from rioters or cops. What did it say about people that it took so little to reduce them to this? What did it say about civilization that it took so little to unravel it?

He was looking for the Grail just like they were—it was true—but he was doing it for Nora, and that set him apart. Once he had her back, they'd deal with the Devil.

The twins flew on, racing through the blazing heat. It was still hot—high nineties for sure—but the wind flowing over them was cooling, and their wings were powerful shields. As they flew, both gained more and more control, and with that control, they gained even more speed.

Before they knew it they were out of Portland. The countryside below was quiet. No people at all it seemed, and no fires. There was farmland. If they didn't know better, they'd have thought all was well with the world down there.

Daphna tried to assess the situation as she flew. It seemed prudent because she found herself having to think less and less about flying as the action became increasingly instinctive. But she couldn't sustain clear thoughts, other than those about her brother being responsible for Branwen having wings. She'd agreed to take her into the clinic when he'd mentioned being righteous—it was true. And it certainly felt righteous to help someone who only wanted to hurt them. There really hadn't been another time since their nightmares had begun when a decision like that had been so clear. But Daphna was sure they would regret it. And she really wasn't so sure Dex was thinking about righteousness at all when it came to helping Branwen. Nora or no Nora, Branwen was Branwen—and Dexter was a boy.

Quinn! Daphna felt for the library book under her wing—and sighed when she found it still safely wedged between two of the many layers of feathers there—feathers that felt like flexible steel. But she didn't want to think about Quinn—not now. Quinn or anything else for that matter, especially the fact that they were going to try to fly all the way to Israel. Fortunately, every time a halfway coherent thought formed, it frayed and flew away on the wind. And she kept hearing the engine of a plane, though every time she jerked around fearfully to find it, expecting to see some Air Force jet shooting missiles at them, there was nothing there. There was nothing for miles around, nothing but blue sky and white clouds.

Mercifully, Daphna eventually found she could feather breathe, even while she flew, and doing so finally put her brother and Branwen and engines and Quinn out of mind. She was flying, and that's all she thought about. She let everything else go.

Somewhere along the line, Dexter had stopped thinking, too. He felt free and light and full of physical power, the likes of which he'd never even imagined. He cut through the wind like a sword. He was a sword, slicing sky.

The twins, only dimly aware of each other, nonetheless rose and fell together on currents they could somehow sense with their feathers. There were layers of air at different temperatures. Without consciously agreeing to do so, they found themselves side-by-side, plunging in and out of low-lying clouds, reveling in the joy of flight. Birds sometimes flew alongside, only to quickly wheel away, dwarfed and shamed, no doubt, by the grandeur of the twins' magnificent wings.

At some point, Dex and Daphna noticed the landscape below had changed. It was dry now. Brown. But Central Oregon passed as quickly as it appeared. And soon enough, they were flying almost too fast to see anything clearly. Towns became blurs, appearing and disappearing, it seemed, with nearly every breathtaking wingstroke.

It wasn't long before they lost all sense of time.

The twins passed over other cities, many cities, large and small, but they paid little attention to them. When they did look, there were helicopters and fires and sirens and looting. Mostly, they didn't look.

They flew.

They just simply flew—over snow-capped mountains and valleys and rivers and towns. They would fly forever, and nothing would ever make them stop.

Until it became obvious that wasn't true. Dr. Lewis, of course, had lied to them about this, too. They began to tire.

Each wingstroke started to feel a little more difficult to execute than the last. The twins' arms and legs grew heavy, and so did their eyes.

Forced to face reality again, Daphna scanned the world below. They'd been flying in the dark for several hours and were approaching a city, a huge one, lit up and spreading out over the horizon like a glittering promise. It gave Daphna hope, though for what, she didn't know. She pointed down at the vast net of lights, and her brother nodded. He knew they'd have to find a place to rest down there.

As they descended, the urban landscape emerged in detail.

When Daphna realized what she was looking at, she pointed, her eyes wide with surprise and pleasure. Dex, to whom the city was still mostly a matrix of fuzzy glows, followed her finger. The ocean? They'd made it all the way to the ocean?

"New York!" Daphna cried. "New York City!"

Dex was amazed to see that she was right. The skyline was unmistakable.

But the city was tearing itself apart.

CHAPTER TWENTY-FOUR
Like the Fourth of July

News of Martial Law did not seem to have made it to the Big Apple because there were thousands—*tens* of thousands—of people on the streets. As far as the twins could tell, there was no police or military presence whatsoever. A clamorous, undifferentiated roar was rising up from the city: the sound of anarchy.

"Dex—where?" Daphna asked, unsure where it might be safe to land. She needed to land. She needed to land *now*.

"There!" Dex cried, pointing toward the ocean. "Follow me!"

"What?" But then Daphna saw what he was aiming for.

The Statue of Liberty.

Daphna flew up alongside her brother, nearly exhausted, and together they approached the famous statue on its little island. There was a balcony around the torch, Daphna saw. She'd never really noticed that before.

It was perfect.

The twins landed on it and immediately collapsed in two spent heaps.

They stayed on their backs for a while, catching their breaths. But at the sound of several explosions, they dragged themselves to their feet to look out at the cityscape.

There was New York, the greatest city in the world, in chaos. Several more explosions went off in different areas. It looked and sounded like the Fourth of July. A few boats were out on the water. Passengers were watching the show.

Holding onto the ledge for support, the twins moved around the torch, looking up at its metal flames as they made their way.

The Statue of Liberty. They were on the *Statue of Liberty*.

There was the ocean, the vast and terrifying obstacle that lay between them and their goal. That is, if the Secret Keeper knew what he was talking about—at least about where the book that was the Grail was hidden, whatever it actually contained.

The twins sank down again with their backs against the torch, looking out at the water.

"Flying," Daphna sighed. "That was the coolest experience of my life."

"Mine too."

"But we didn't get far enough, Dex. Assuming we can fly again in the morning, we'll only have a week before Dr. Fludd and Nora and Quinn's parents and Wren are lost forever. And what if we can't make it over the ocean? Our wings are obviously not that strong. And if we do, how are we supposed to find Israel? And if we do, how are we supposed to—"

"I think it's six."

"What?"

"I think we only have six days. The holidays start in the evening, so—"

"Oh, my God! You're right. Yom Kippur starts—six evenings from now! Six! What are we going to—?"

"Do you still have that library book?"

Daphna had forgotten about it again. She reached back tentatively under her wing, terrified she'd lost it, ready to hurl herself into the ocean if so. But there it was, safe and sound. Relieved, she pulled the book out and got right to reading.

But she was so tired, and it was dark—though the stars were bright and her eyes were strong.

Dex just lay there on his back. His wings were useless, his arms and legs like jelly. "Let's just skip the background stuff for once, shall we?" he said through a giant yawn. He eyes slowly closed. The sounds of mayhem coming from the city were almost soothing.

"Okay," Daphna said. "Good idea. *Dex,* don't fall asleep. You've got to help me stay—"

She looked away from her brother, disgusted. He was already asleep. But Daphna couldn't manage to read more than few lines before her own eyes were too heavy to hold open. The words bent and blurred when she tried to read with them half closed. She wondered if Dex's Scotopic Sensitivity Syndrome made reading something like—

But that was the end of Daphna's thoughts on the matter because now she was asleep, too.

CHAPTER TWENTY-FIVE
The Book of Death

"Ah, Daphna—" Dex nudged her with his foot.

Daphna opened her eyes, then leapt to her feet. The sun was too high. They'd slept half the day! She hadn't tried to reach Quinn at all. *Not even once!* She hadn't learned a single thing! How could she do that to him? What was wrong with her? "Dex!" she cried, but then she realized what Dex was staring at out on the water.

"I have no idea," Dex whispered. He'd woken up a few minutes earlier and gotten groggily to his feet to find—this.

There were hundreds and hundreds, perhaps a *thousand,* boats on the water, boats of every kind: motor boats, sailboats, yachts large and small, even canoes and kayaks. They floated side-by-side bumping gunnels in the softly sloshing sea.

Every one of them was crowded with people simply standing and staring up at the twins in stunned silence. Most held binoculars pressed to their eyes.

The silence was palpable, like a field of energy. Utterly dumbfounded, the twins walked slowly around the torch looking out at the thousands of eyes looking at them. The island was completely surrounded.

When they turned their attention to the city, the twins realized all was quiet.

Dexter put up a hand and waved.

The people responded with a sudden burst of wild, almost ecstatic, cheering.

"What is going on?" Daphna asked out of the side of her mouth. How could they know—? And neither of us have our phones."

"Hold on," Dex said. And before Daphna could ask what he meant, he took off, leaping from the balcony into full flight.

There was a collective gasp from all directions, a prolonged intake that seemed almost to tug the air.

"Dexter!"

Dex landed on the deck of a pleasure craft. The people on deck, men and women and children, all backed away, staring at him with what could only be called awe. For a moment Dexter could only stare back, entranced by the adoration.

They loved him.

"My name is—" Dex started to say, but someone interrupted him, a small boy with red cheeks and windblown hair. It was the boy Dex had flown over to.

"Mr. Angel?" he said. "Are you gonna save us from the Bad Man?"

Dex swallowed a lump in his throat. "Ah, yeah," he said. "I mean, yes. We are going to—We *shall* save you. Do you think I could borrow that?"

The boy looked over at a woman who had to be his mother. She nodded, so he held out the cell phone Dex had spotted. The boy's eyes said he trusted Dex with all his heart.

"Thank you," Dex said. He burst into the air and flew back to his sister.

"Dex!" Daphna said when he landed. "What the heck—?"

Dex showed her the phone.

"Oh." Daphna took it from him, gruffly. "Good idea." She was having trouble taking her eyes off of all the eyes on her. The avid gaze of all those eyes was causing heat to pour off her face. How was she supposed to live up to what they thought she was? She wanted to hide. Instead, she tapped the phone to open a search engine. When it came up, she loaded a news site.

The headline filled the screen:

ANGELS IN AMERICA

Below was a photo of the twins standing where they were now—but the shot was taken last night with the sun's last rays upon their still outstretched wings. Someone out on the water must have snapped it.

Daphna swiped the page down a bit and read out loud: "'Two more angels have been spotted—' Two *more?*"

"Branwen."

"Oh, God. Dexter!"

"Keep reading."

After a deep breath, Daphna continued: "Two more angels have been spotted in America, and as the news and photos spread around the world, so did hope that the presumed imminent war against Evil, against the Devil himself according to a number of religious authorities, will not be fought alone. The first angel, a female of astonishing beauty—"

Daphna took another deep breath.

"Keep reading."

"—was spotted briefly yesterday flying over Portland, Oregon, giving rise to speculation that what is looming is in fact Armageddon, the final battle during which, according to some Christians, Jesus will return to Earth. There are myriad claims of a hoax, especially because missing billionaire occultist and self-promoter Virgil Durante made similar claims about one of the two new angels, Dexter Wax. He broadcasted pictures of the boy appearing to have a halo during the plague scare. Nonetheless, church leaders worldwide urge their flocks to prepare. The Vatican issued a statement confirming that the "End of Days" is upon us, citing the appearance of these angles as 'irrefutable proof.'"

"Right," Dex said. "Of course."

Daphna looked at him, but did not respond. She went back to reading: "Rioting in every city, it seems, but Jerusalem, has all but ceased at this news, as has the search for the mysterious "Golden Book." The prevailing theory is that it is the Book of Death, which some claim the Devil himself wrote to make man mortal. It is feared that he seeks to drastically shorten life, or even to extinguish it completely. The two new angels pictured here have been identified as Dexter and Daphna Wax, who, many now assume, were the source of the cure for the plague rather than its cause, though officials at Oregon Health Science University have refused to comment on the matter. Dr. Roberta Fludd, who'd been given credit for the cure, is missing at this time. Research into the twin's past reveals all sorts of unexplained gaps in their lineage, giving credence to the theory that they have been among us for many generations, waiting for this time. Also missing from the Oregon hospital is Arthur Picarelli, the man whose claims upon recovering from a lengthy coma began this entire—"

Daphna handed the phone back. She'd read enough.

"*The Book of the Dead?*" Dex sighed. He'd only been half listening while staring out over the sea of—worshipers?

Daphna joined her brother, gazing at all the people still standing on their boats, still staring up at them in expectant silence. "This is all—" she said. "I don't know what to—The entire world thinks we're angels! They're practically *praying* to us, Dex. This can't be a good thing."

"You always wanted to be popular, right?" Dex said, watching the red-cheeked boy waving to him. Then he turned to Daphna and added, "Looks like your ships have come in."

"We need to go," Daphna said, ignoring this. She didn't have time to decide whether Dex was being sarcastic or not. She'd never felt so profoundly uncomfortable in her life—but it didn't matter. It was what it was, and there was simply no time to dwell on irrelevant feelings. "We have five days left," she added as the implications of their oversleeping began to set in. "And even if we knew what direction to fly—" she groaned, looking out at the open waters, "What if we get tired over the middle of the ocean? We didn't really think this through enough, Dex. We should've—"

Dex had no time for whining and moaning. He felt full of boundless, bottomless energy now—more boundless and bottomless energy than he felt yesterday. They'd obviously slept that long for a reason. He took off again, launching himself straight out over the water. There was another burst of cheering from the boats below, a loud and prolonged burst at what surely looked like the angels springing into action. The cheering thrilled Dexter. He rose up out of his flight path and executed a loop that took him swiftly back over the bobbing boats. He swooped over to the pleasure craft and handed the phone back to its wide-eyed owner, then launched himself back into the clear morning sky. A roar followed him, sending him back out over the water feeling invincible as he slammed his wings against the wind.

Daphna shook her head at her brother's gratuitous display. She wasn't going to follow him this time.

He'd come back, and they'd figure out a rational plan, one that didn't involve drowning.

But he was already almost out of sight, even her angel-powered sight.

Daphna turned and looked down at all the adoring faces on the boats. They were focused on her now, full of anxious anticipation.

"Go! Go! Go!" someone cheered.

Daphna sighed.

The crowd quickly picked up the chant. "Go! Go! Go!"

She took off.

And despite herself, the cheering made her smile.

CHAPTER TWENTY-SIX
The Slowly Spreading Stain

Dexter did not speak to his sister for the next six hours, though he made sure every once in a while that she was in the vicinity. He preferred to imagine that he was going it alone. Wasn't the time coming when he'd have to, once and for all? He and Daphna had done so much for each other since their lives fell apart. It was staggering how much they'd accomplished. They loved each other—Dex didn't, and would never, doubt that. But the hard truth was that, despite the considerable contributions he'd made to their unlikely discoveries and frequent dramatic escapes, he needed her more than she needed him. If one of them ever made things harder, it was always him. *I handled myself with Durante well enough on my own, though,* Dex thought, ignoring the minor detail that, if Daphna hadn't come for him, he would have suffocated to death in one of the morose billionaire's display cases. But he hadn't been afraid of dying, though that was because he thought Daphna was dead at the time and no longer cared about anything. That was obviously not a way to live your life long-term, not if you value it. And he'd finally seen the value of it when he met Nora.

All brothers and sisters eventually parted ways. They found partners. *Real* partners. *Life* partners. Somewhere over the ocean in the middle of the world, Dexter realized that while Daphna was his history, Nora was his future.

At some point, Dex pushed this all away so he could concentrate solely on the sensational feeling the flapping of his wings produced, to savor the movement of his miraculous new muscles. The sheer pleasure of his power was overwhelming. It dwarfed what he could do yesterday. He knew he could be nothing but a blur to anyone who saw him, an ivory streak in the sky. But there was no one to see him but the fish. He watched his reflection on the water below surfing the waves.

At times Dex thought he heard an engine, but never spotted any sort of plane. He was absolutely certain he could fly all the way to—Well, he was just somehow sure they'd find their way to Israel. Daphna's sense-of-direction had never failed her. He wasn't done relying on her—that was clear enough. Anyway, they were born in Jerusalem.

They were birds returning to their nests.

Dexter flew on, hour after hour after hour, exalting in flight, but just like yesterday there came a moment, a sudden, unambiguous moment when he had no choice but to acknowledge what a fool he was, what a fool he'd always been—the moment he felt the first twinge of fatigue. It was just the slightest thing, just the shadow of a feeling. He immediately began searching for land. They would need somewhere to rest. Soon.

Or, he'd killed them.

Daphna had been looking for land for the last hour. She wanted to kill Dex for doing this to them, but she knew she was to blame as well for letting the crowd's adoration cloud her judgment. She'd also felt so strong setting out, and she'd ignored the voice in her head telling her to turn back while there was still time.

Dex would have come back.

Or so went Daphna's thinking for a while. Eventually, she had to concede that a small part of her thought he just might not have come back, that he was on his own mission that rendered her mostly irrelevant. Things were bad between them, she knew. Really bad. Worse, she had no idea how to make them better.

Daphna started laboring well before Dex did and had fallen quite far behind him. A heaviness overtook her wings, the same heaviness that rendered her unconscious last night. She hadn't read enough of that library book! And now it was looking increasingly like she'd never get the chance.

Quinn, Daphna thought as she drifted down toward the water. She closed her eyes.

"I'm sorry!" Dex cried.

Daphna opened her eyes.

"I'm sorry!" Dex was right next to her, struggling every bit as badly as she was.

All around them—three hundred and sixty degrees around them—was water.

Daphna touched down on the surface of the sea. The cold was shocking, but she wrapped herself in her wings and was suddenly warm again. She floated on her back.

Dex touched down a moment later and wrapped himself round as well.

Brother and sister looked at each other as they floated side-by-side.

"We'll rest this way," Daphna said, relieved to see that drowning might not be inevitable. "We'll sleep, and then we'll be strong again. I'm starv—"

Something fell into the water nearby by, sending up a small but frightening splash.

"What was that?" Daphna's heart was in her throat.

"Oh, no."

Rising up through the water from the spot of the splash was something red.

Blood.

"Something got attacked!" Daphna wailed.

"Oh, no—"

Dark shapes were in the water, circling the slowly spreading stain.

It took Daphna a moment to comprehend what she was seeing, but comprehend she did.

The twins screamed together: "Sharks!"

CHAPTER TWENTY-SEVEN
Plane Sight

Panicking, the twins flapped wildly out of the water, but neither had the strength to get more than a few feet into the air.

Yes, they were sharks. Dozens of them were converging on the blood—or whatever was bleeding.

"Dex!" Daphna shrieked. "I can't do this for very—!"

"Look!" Dex shouted, pointing to the sky.

A plane.

It seemed to have appeared from out of nowhere, almost directly overhead.

"Come back!" Daphna screamed as it headed into the distance.

But wait—it seemed to be swinging round.

"It's coming back!" Dex cheered.

Daphna squinted at it, straining her powerful eyes. The plane was white and had big blue letters painted on its side. "That's Hebrew!" she cried.

Suddenly filled with energy—adrenaline anyway—Dex willed himself into the sky.

"Wait!" Daphna called after him, still laboring just to hover above the sharks, which were now in a feeding frenzy a few feet below her shoes. "It's too much of a coincidence! Something's not—!"

"It's *him!*" Dex shouted, looking down. "The Secret Keeper! They're trying to help us!"

Daphna was sure he was right. This plane had to be the source of the engine noise she kept hearing. They'd somehow been following them the whole time, watching to see if they needed help. They must have figured out how to get permission to fly.

Anyway, Daphna thought, whoever it was couldn't be less welcoming than the sharks. She willed her wings to lift her into the air behind her brother.

Both twins felt their muscles burning badly as they flapped higher into the sky; it was amazing how motivating sharks could be. They found the strength to gain the altitude they needed. The plane was getting close, so they circled around to meet it from the side. Dex looked to Daphna, who watched it carefully, calculating distances and speed in her mind. She was guessing.

"Now!" she cried.

The twins took off, flapping for all they were worth. They cut a path perpendicular the plane as it roared toward them.

It was there.

The twins dove at the wing. Dex managed to grab hold of it. Daphna, right next to her brother, got a grip on him. He dragged her arm until it clutched the cold metal of the wing.

They were there, but the effort took all they had. Exhausted, all the twins could do was hold on with their heads turned sideways to protect them from the battering winds.

Why weren't they being helped? How do you board a moving jet?

"It's blue!" Daphna screamed over the wind. When she saw the look of incomprehension in her Dexter's eyes, she screamed, "The plane! It's blue now!"

Dex saw that this was true. The plane was all blue, a blue identical to the blue sky around it.

So that's why they never spotted it.

"It's a screen!" Dex shouted. The Hebrew letters were gone. The entire shell of the plane was a video screen. It had gone white so they could see it, but now it didn't want to be seen.

"I can't hold on much longer!" Daphna cried. She was going to let go. She was going fall into the ocean again.

"Doors!" Dex cried.

A hatch over their wing was opening up.

A large man with a pronounced cleft in his chin, steadied by an even larger man, reached out and grabbed Dex by the wrists, then yanked him into the plane. Daphna slid closer to the hatch so she could be reached. Moments later, she was hauled inside, too.

The hatch was closed, and the violent noise of the wind was suddenly gone.

"They're not wearing black," Daphna observed, though that didn't really mean much. Slowly, weakly, she got to her feet. Her arms were dead weight, and her wings drooped like wilted flowers. But then she saw that her wrists were bloody. *What the heck?* she said. Had she been cut—or bitten?

Dex was up too and also trying to comprehend the blood all over his wrists and forearms.

"Dex, look—"

There was a large bucket by the hatch full of raw, bloody meat.

The twins looked at the two men, who looked back at them blankly. Their hands were covered in blood.

"You threw the meat to *attract* the sharks?" Dex asked. "Then came back for us?"

"That way," the cleft-chin guy said, pointing his chin into the fuselage.

The twins turned around to see that they weren't in any ordinary kind of jet. All the seats had been replaced by couches and desks—but there was a large open area set up as another little operating room. A man, even larger than the first two, a positively massive man with no shirt on, was standing with his back to them, looking down at a body on an operating table.

The body was Branwen's.

Slowly, he turned round, giving the twins two more shocks.

The first was what lay in his oversized hands: a set of desiccated wings. They were lifeless and black. They were Branwen's, and they were dead.

The second was his face.

"But—" the twins both gasped when they looked up to see it, "you're dead."

"Hardly," said Virgil Durante. "And don't worry," he added. "Neither is your pretty little friend here. At least not yet."

Before the twins could respond to this, needles were jammed into the back of their necks.

CHAPTER TWENTY-EIGHT
Some Nether World

Dex! Please hurry, Dex! I'm so scared. There's a door. There's a door here, in his library. Behind it—It leads to the Realm of Dead Souls! When he opens it we feel the emptiness! It's so cold, Dex! I'm so afraid!

"Nora!" Dex cried. He was nowhere, floating in some netherworld. It was dark. He couldn't see anything. No Letters, no Light. Nothing.

Hurry, Dex! I need you. I need you so much! I'm sorry if I'm selfish, but I want to live! With you!

Nora's sobbing filled the darkness.

"I'm trying, Nora," Dex sobbed back. "I'm trying so hard."

I know you are. You're special, Dex. You're different, even from your sister. You have anger, righteous anger, and it will give you strength to do what must be done.

"I'm coming!" Dex promised. "I'm coming to set you free!"

Daphna!

"Quinn! Where are you? Quinn! I can't see you!" Daphna was nowhere—nowhere real. There was only dark, impenetrable dark.

I'm here, Daphna. I'm back in my body, alive! Don't worry about me. The book—focus on the book. Everyone is relying on you. Please bring my parents back. Please!

"I will Quinn! I will! And I will see you soon!"

I know you will. I know you are the one who can destroy the Dragon. You have a level head. You'll do what's needed. You always do what's right.

"But, Quinn, I don't always know what's right! I need your help! Can you tell me what the book really is?"

I'm think I'm waking up, Daphna! I love—!

"Quinn! Quinn! I love you too!"

Dex felt like he was in bed. For a moment, he indulged the fantasy that it had been a dream—*all of it*—and that at any moment he would wake up and leave the house before his father got home from Turkey with The Book of Nonsense. But what was the point? He could hear the engine of the plane.

Dexter opened his eyes and saw a blurry version of his sister standing next to the couch he realized he was lying on. She was staring at him with red-rimmed eyes, which meant she'd been crying. On the other hand, the flecks in her irises seemed animated like they sometimes did when she was passionate about something. But then her whole face went wavy and weird.

"They followed us," Daphna said. "They were waiting for us to get exhausted so we couldn't fight back. They threw the meat into the water to guarantee we'd have to take their help."

"They're gone, aren't they?"

"I'm so sorry," Daphna said with fat tears rising in her eyes. "Dex—"

"He took them, didn't he? He took my wings. Durante *collected* them."

"Yes," Daphna confirmed, looking down. "But it's not exactly Durante."

"What?" Dex was losing her. The wooziness was shutting his brain down. *"Wait,"* he said, "you still have yours?"

"It's his brother. His identical twin brother."

Dex heard this. He understood it. But he was spared the necessity of reacting to it because, mercifully, the netherworld took him back.

CHAPTER TWENTY-NINE
The Experience of a Lifetime

"You should have taken mine!" Daphna shouted. "Dex—he needs—Dex? *Are you awake again?*"

He was.

"Dex! Are you back?"

"Why *did* you take mine?"

The giant of a man standing beside Daphna looked absolutely, one hundred percent, like Virgil Durante. Granite jaw. Refrigerator box build. A perfect match.

Except this version had wings on his bare, muscle-bound back.

Dexter's wings.

"We haven't been formally introduced," the man said, approaching the couch with a hairy, caveman hand extended. Dexter declined to take it. "I'm Homer Durante," the man said, anyway. "I'm sorry I didn't ask for the wings, but something told me you might not be too keen on handing them over. You seemed to be the stronger flyer, and while I suspect that had nothing to do with the wings, per say, I figured, you know, just in case."

"What do you want with them, anyway?" Daphna demanded.

"Want?" Durante asked, as if shocked by the absurdity of the question. "What do I *want*?" he asked again. "Either of you ever jump out of a plane?"

The twins looked at each other, confused by the question.

"No," Dex answered for them.

"I have," Durante said. "And off of cliffs. And a skyscraper."

"Okay..." Daphna said.

"And I've run with the bulls. And I've eaten Siberian Tiger, a Ploughshare Tortoise, and a square watermelon. I met every living president. I've been with—never mind that. I've taken every drug known to man. Take my word for it, I've done it all, *experienced* it all—"

"Except death," Daphna said, finally getting the point.

"But by the looks of things down below," Durante said, "that might not be long off. I guess my brother's swansong was a doozy. You'll have to tell me about that sometime."

The twins looked at each other, incredulous.

"The *purpose* of life," Durante continued, throwing up his tree trunk arms, "is to *live* life, to properly *experience* it. It's the only way to honor it. It's the only way to *deserve* it! And *this* experience," he said, moving his wings a bit, "might just top them all. I don't sound like my brother now, do I?" he asked, flashing a smile full of teeth that looked like little picket fences. "He was always the serious one." Durante winked and added, "But there's always a good twin and a bad twin, no?" He laughed at the distress this drew on both Dexter's and Daphna's faces.

Dex found he could sit up. His back felt like it was badly sunburned, as if the skin were brittle and stretched thin, but he otherwise felt fine. Did Daphna feel okay? She looked fully recovered. When did that happen, and why hadn't she immediately torn this guy to pieces? No matter how big he was, as a human, he'd have been no match for her with wings. Now it was too late. Dex glared at Daphna to communicate his anger and confusion, and she seemed to get the message.

"Mr. Durante has promised to take us to Jerusalem," she said, pointedly. *"If* we help teach him how to use the wings. We're almost there, Dex. It's almost ten a.m. here. And if we don't help," she added even more forcefully, "he's going to kill Branwen. My *best friend,* Branwen."

Dex almost laughed at this, but the sudden intensity in Daphna's eyes told him to play along. He looked over across the plane and saw Branwen. She was sitting in one of a half-dozen leather passenger chairs, looking well beyond haggard. And yet she was still so pretty—so *Branwen.* It was hard to believe, but undeniably true. She was awake and staring right back at him with unblinking eyes. The slightest turn of her lip made Dex think she knew exactly what he was thinking, that she knew he'd only suggested taking her in to the doctor because she enthralled him like she did everyone else. Dex assumed Daphna thought the same thing, despite his claim about wanting to do the righteous thing. Fact was, he wasn't sure which it was.

"Yes, I see," Dex said, turning back to Daphna, understanding now that she wanted Durante to think he had leverage over them until they got to Jerusalem. "Okay."

"I might have been a bit overzealous when we picked her up," Durante said, looking at Branwen. "I think I'll keep her—a pretty pet—but who knows how much time we have left? Anyway, we basically just tore the wings off, and they rather unceremoniously died. Luckily you two showed up on the news and gave us another shot. If these babies don't work out," he said, looking at his new wings, "I'm sure the third time will be the charm."

"They'll work," the twins promised, both glancing nervously at Branwen, who didn't say a word. She was staring at Daphna now, her eyes calm waters but with something scarier than sharks swimming just below the surface.

"In fact," Daphna said, turning to Durante, "there's not much we need to tell you. They work right away. You don't have to do anything special at all. An instinct just sort of takes over. You put yourself out there, and you're flying. It's amazing."

Durante's eyes got increasingly large as Daphna spoke.

"It's the first burst that you'll never forget," Dex put in. "It's like a volcano exploding inside of you. It's like you are superhuman."

"You *are* superhuman," Daphna said. "It's the experience of a lifetime."

"Of a million lifetimes," Dex added. "I wouldn't wait a single minute to try it out if I were you."

Durante turned to his goons. "Now," he said. "I'm going to do it now."

"But—" one of the goons hesitantly objected, "perhaps we should wait until we touch down. We're over Jerusalem now."

"Actually," Daphna said, "way up in the sky is the best place to start. Um, because—" But then she faltered.

"Room," Dex explained. "Lots more room to spread your wings."

"Exactly!"

"Now," Durante repeated, this time in a voice that clearly meant the decision was final.

The goon nodded.

Dex and Daphna exchanged another look as the lumbering giant followed his lackeys to the hatch at the front of the plane. The twins trailed nervously behind.

A goon opened the hatch, and everyone reached for something to hold on to when the roaring winds tried to snatch them right out into the sky. Durante, an immovable object, hadn't grabbed anything. He stepped forward and stood right on the edge, only then putting a hand up to steady himself. His wings twitched with anticipation on his broad back. On him, they hardly looked oversized.

"Awesome," Durante said. He turned to his goon and added, "If this works, take the other set of wings—and make sure the twins are dead before I get back."

Then he spun round and leapt out of the plane.

The twins both heard Durante's order, but it didn't matter because, just as they expected, after one powerful but awkward semi-flap of his wings, Durante twisted a bit, then fell in a heap onto the wing of the plane.

He bounced on the metal surface, which clanged a bit in protest of his weight. The mountain of a man flailed his arms and legs—but it was useless, even for him.

The engine sucked him right in.

CHAPTER THIRTY
A Shimmering City of White

"Go!" Daphna screamed, grabbing her brother. She shoved him toward the open hatch. The goons were frozen, paralyzed by the gruesome disaster. None of them seemed even to notice the twins pushing right past them.

Dexter was simultaneously thrilled and horrified by the turn of events, and the combination prevented him from reacting to what Daphna was doing until she'd forced him out of the plane and he found himself hurtling through open sky. "DAAAAAAPH—!" he screamed, but suddenly she was there. She'd swooped under him, and he was on her back.

They passed into a cloud and everything was fog for moment, but then they dropped out of it.

There, spread out majestically below them, was a shimmering city of white.

It was the city where they'd been born.

It was Jerusalem.

It was hot here, as hot as it had been in Portland before the sky broke open. The twins could scarcely breathe without singeing their lungs. Even the wind rushing over them was of little help.

Dex and Daphna did their best to ignore it as they soared over the city, looking for—they weren't sure. It spread out below them like an ancient model: sun bleached geometrical stone structures packed close together but scored by narrow streets. The landscape around was dry brown desert, punctuated by patches of shocking green.

The twins heard gunfire. Explosions and gunfire.

Moments later they'd descended enough to see military trucks speeding in all directions. Sirens were wailing. People were running helter-skelter in the streets. They were swinging pipes and throwing rocks and firing small arms.

The Holy City was at war.

This did not surprise the twins. What did surprise them was that, as people caught sight of Daphna, they stopped swinging pipes and throwing rocks and shooting guns.

Daphna swooped and circled, making herself visible to everyone she could.

The amazing result was that there in the alleys, the streets, and the public squares of Jerusalem, combatants began to lay down their weapons. Some dropped to their knees, some bowed. Still others went right down on their faces. Regardless, the intentions of one and all were clear: to pray.

Dex had a death grip on his sister's back, but she seemed to be having no trouble supporting his weight. He shouted into her ear, "They must not have believed we were actually—!"

"There!" Daphna cried, pointing into the distance.

Dex saw what she saw: a glittering golden dome in the middle of a large stone square.

The Temple Mount.

It was a long stone rectangle boxed in by trees and protected by imposing stone walls. A firefight was raging among the trees. Men in olive military uniforms under bulging protective vests were shooting at each other with clattering machine guns.

"Who are they?" Dex shouted. "They all look the same!"

"Muslim and Israeli guards, I think!" Daphna shouted back. "They both have holy sites here! But I'll take care of it!"

Daphna swooped over the Mount's outer walls, then around the tree line, showing herself to one and all. She knew she'd been seen by everyone when the shooting finally stopped.

Satisfied, she landed on the steps of the Dome of the Rock and let Dexter slide off her back. Soldiers were walking out of the trees, approaching with wonder in their eyes.

"Tell them to lose the guns," Dex hissed out of the side of his mouth. *"And to scram."*

Daphna managed to croak out, "Go from this place." But then she added, more confidently, "Leave your weapons and go!"

There was an awful moment when nothing happened—because of course who knew if any of them understood English. Both twins feared for their lives.

But then the men set down their guns, turned, and began to leave the Mount.

Five minutes later, Dex and Daphna were alone, surrounded by small but terrifying piles of automatic weapons, standing on the steps of the Dome of the Rock.

They'd made it to the Temple Mount.

And they had it all to themselves.

Or maybe they didn't.

"Daphna, look."

There was a man—not a soldier, or not an ordinary soldier—who seemed to have suddenly materialized from medieval times. He was clad in chainmail under a white robe adorned with a large red cross. A long sword hung by his side in silver scabbard. He was standing next to a stone fountain, which looked to be just about right in the middle of the Mount.

"I don't think he's a Mason," Daphna said. "At least he's not dressed like one."

The man waved them over.

The twins hesitated, looked at each other, then back at the—*knight?*

He waved them over again, more urgently now.

"Let's see what he wants," Daphna said. "But we better be careful. Remember: Mr. Brown said the Colors couldn't try to break in here because they'd all get killed."

"They have Qeres."

Daphna swallowed a lump in her throat, but nodded, so the twins cautiously approached the fountain, which they saw was dry. It was ringed by a low stone wall topped by green fencing.

The knight, bearded, broad shouldered, and surly-looking, inspected the twins when they reached him. His dark eyes settled on Daphna, and he nodded to her. "We've been waiting for you," he said in English, but with a British accent.

"You're a Templar," Dex guessed.

Daphna turned to Dex, remembering that the Secret Keeper had mentioned them.

"The Knights Templar," Dex elaborated, "protectors of the Grail."

The Templar bowed slightly.

"Where did you come from?" Dex asked, wondering how the soldiers could have failed to spot him in that getup.

Instead of answering, the Templar looked around, so the twins did too. The Dome of the Rock was in front of them, the smaller mosque behind. Both sat silently in the blistering heat.

No sounds at all came from beyond the walls.

Evidently satisfied, the Templar stepped down to the low wall that encircled the fountain. Rather stiffly, he went down on a knee, then pressed one of the round, seemingly decorative mountings on it. Then he stood back up.

For a moment, nothing happened, but then the wall began to slide apart along the stones on which it sat. The Templar waved the twins to follow him toward the actual fountain, which looked like a bowl with a scepter in it. He stepped up onto the base and held the top of the scepter, so the twins did the same.

The base of the fountain shook under their feet. For a moment, the twins feared another earthquake, but then they realized what was happening: the fountain was sinking into the ground. Dexter and Daphna held their breath as darkness enveloped them, save for a shrinking disk of light over their heads. The sounds of gears creaking and turning filled the shaft as they descended, until, finally, they stopped. The Templar stepped from the fountain onto a dimly lit stone floor. The twins followed.

They were in some kind of cave. The heat was, mercifully, gone. It smelled of cold, dry earth.

"Step back please," the Templar said.

The twins did so, then watched the fountain slowly rise back over them, blotting out the little light it had allowed in.

It was now completely dark.

Daphna reached for her brother, but lights suddenly came on. Electric lights, mounted on the stone walls.

The twins looked around, not sure what to make of what really wasn't a cave at all. It was a room.

"I thought it would be—messier," Daphna said. "I assumed there'd be lots of—old stuff."

"Over time," the Templar said, "we have painstakingly excavated a vast system of store rooms, cisterns, tunnels, and corridors." He stepped into a tunnel and began walking through it.

"Another labyrinth," Dex said, following him in. The world was a labyrinth as far as he was concerned.

And that's exactly what the twins found themselves being led through. The ground they walked on was polished and smooth—concrete had been poured. They passed in and out of empty rooms in silence for a while, just looking.

It turned out that not all the rooms and chambers were equally finished. Some had dirt walls and holes in the ground. Those had pikes and shovels and sifters lying around.

"Wait a second," Dex said, stopping to look down into one the holes as they passed it. "You're not protecting the Grail, are you? You're *looking* for it. You don't know where it is. You probably don't even know *what* it is."

"We know both," the Templar replied. The twins waited for more, so he added, "There are many other treasures hidden here as well." Then he led them through a passage they all had to turn sideways to get through.

When they emerged from it, Dex and Daphna found themselves in a large cavern. A dozen more Templars were there, standing around something on the ground.

The men, all in similar armor and robes, stepped aside to let their apparent leader approach with the twins. All eyes were on Daphna, though, wide and wondering.

The something they'd been standing around was large slab on the cavern floor, a long uneven stone. It had to be a dozen feet in length and almost that wide. It was either sitting on the ground or sticking up through it from below.

"Behold," the Templar said, "that which was made with no hands."

"That which—*what?*" Daphna asked.

"What sits above is a prop to please the masses," he said, pointing to the cave's ceiling. Here you stand before the first part of this world called into being by God. *This* is the true stone—the *Foundation Stone.*

CHAPTER THIRTY-ONE
The Foundation Stone

"Stone," the twins both echoed, looking to each other.

"Underneath the Foundation Stone," the Templar said, "lies the Well of Souls. It is there the souls of the dead will gather for the Final Judgment. We believe the Grail is hidden there."

"So," Dex said, "have you *looked?*"

"They can't," Daphna explained. "The Stone might be in the Holy of Holies. Remember, you can't go in there unless you are a—*Cohen Ga*—a High Priest. They're worried about being struck dead." She turned to the Templar and asked, "How long have you known this was actually down here?"

"Centuries," the Templar said. "While above they kill each other to control this land, we remain below, guarding the Well, waiting for someone able to enter it."

"Like an angel," Dex said.

"The End Times are upon us," the Templar declared. "Therefore it is no surprise that you have come. We have been expecting you. The only thing that will save us from the Devil is the Stone."

"But just finding it," Daphna started to protest, "doesn't mean you'll be able to—*Wait,* the *what* will save us? Do you mean the Foundation Stone?"

"You test us," the Templar said, nodding as if to indicate he expected nothing less. "We know what the Grail is," he assured Daphna. "We know it is not a cup, nor a plate, nor a book. We know it is merely a stone, an ordinary stone desperately picked up from the ground by Joseph of Arimathea and used to collect our Savior's blood as it ran from his wounds."

"During the crucifixion," Dex said, and the Templar nodded again.

The twins looked at each other and sighed.

But it made some sense to Daphna. "Set in stone,"

she said. "Why would he have come with a cup? A book is reasonable, if he was hoping to take down last words, but maybe he had nothing." Then why were they sent to find a golden book?

"What does it do?" Dex asked the Templar.

"The Stone," he said, "transfers the divine, eternal life-force of our Savior's blood to all who touch it—to all *believers* who touch it."

"The Philosopher's Stone!" Daphna cried. "This is where *that* story comes from!"

"We can wait no longer!" the Templar declared, both his voice and color rising. "You must lift the Stone!"

Daphna hadn't really processed the idea that the Templars were waiting for *her* to risk entering the Holy of Holies. "Wait!" she cried, stalling. "Has *anyone* tried? Just, you know, to experiment? Maybe someone who didn't believe in—what you believe?"

"We have never allowed such blasphemy!" the Templar roared. "You will move the stone! Now!"

Daphna panicked, but then she realized they couldn't forcer her, not with her strength.

"Go ahead," Dex said. "These morons have no idea what they're talking about. The Grail is not a *stone*. It's *set* in stone. They—"

"But Dex, what if it was really 'set *on* stone'? Blood can set on stone."

"We do not fear you," the Templar warned. With a sudden jerk of his arm, he unsheathed his sword, which was dripping a clear liquid. Before the twins could think, he had it pressed to Daphna's throat.

"Don't!" Dex begged.

Daphna put her hands up, breathing hard now, trying not to panic at the strong tarragon smell of the Qeres. "Okay!" she said. "I'll do it! I'll do it!"

The Templar lowered his sword, but just as suddenly it was at Dexter's throat and his hands were up.

"I said I'd do it!" Daphna shouted. She turned to the Stone and looked down at it, trembling with fear. How could she take this risk with Quinn awake again? What choice did she have with her brother's life at stake?

Daphna squatted down, trying to buy herself time to think, to avoid having to make the very choice she'd dreaded.

She feather breathed.

She reached a trembling hand out to the Stone.

She feather breathed.

It looked like any sort of ordinary stone. Could it really be the first part of the world created by God?

Daphna tried to steady her hand as she lowered it to the Stone. Cool air seemed to rise from its surface.

She feather breathed.

She didn't know what to do.

"Daphna!" Dex cried.

But it was too late.

Someone shoved her.

Daphna desperately flapped her wings, but there just wasn't time to save herself. She fell sprawled out onto the Stone. It was cold on her hands and cheek. She tensed for—

Nothing.

Nothing happened.

Long sighs sounded around the room. Then came a palpable swelling of excitement.

"I told you," Dex said.

"Are you strong enough to lift it?" the Templar asked as Daphna climbed back onto the cavern floor. She didn't look at Dexter's eyes, but saw the sword was still at his throat.

Daphna squatted once again, then put both hands on the edge of the rough, impossibly ancient stone.

After one more breath, she began to lift it up.

CHAPTER THIRTY-TWO
The Well of Souls

The sound of rock tearing from rock echoed powerfully in the cavern as Daphna freed the Foundation Stone. It wasn't flat on the bottom. In fact, it bulged underneath quite significantly. Still, incredibly, though it had to weigh many thousands of pounds, it wasn't hard to lift.

"It's out! It's out!" the Templar cried, bending over to look into the hole being exposed underneath. Daphna rotated the massive stone away and set it down.

Now all the Templars were gathered around the hole, peering wide-eyed into the darkness below, though not one dared to lean over the edge even the slightest bit. Dex had been pushed forward and was beside Daphna now, wiping blood off his neck. The cut was minor.

"Can you see anything?" the Templar asked Daphna.

Daphna squinted, letting her powerful eyes penetrate the gloom of the Well of Souls.

"I see it!" she cried. "I see the Philosopher's Stone!"

"Where? Where is it!" the Templar demanded.

"It's a small stone," Daphna said, "a flat, roundish stone, glowing gold, way down below." She looked directly into her brother's eyes as she said this, but he already knew she was lying. He flicked his eyes at his feet, so she looked down.

The tip of Dex's shoe was over the lip of the hole—into the Well. And he wasn't dead in body or soul. He slid it back.

"The ground is long and sloping," Daphna announced. "It looks like a ramp."

"We must see if the passage is safe for humans to enter," the Templar declared, raising his sword to Dexter once again.

Before anyone forced him to, Dex jumped into

the hole.

Daphna saw her brother swallowed up by darkness. For a moment, the cavern echoed with the sounds of his body sliding on smooth stone. But then the sliding sounds stopped.

There was silence.

And then there were blood-curdling screams. Dexter sounded as if he were being flayed alive.

The Templars, who'd been straining to see what they could see, all jolted upright.

Dex shrieked and wailed.

"Dex!" Daphna cried. "Dex! *Dex!*"

There was a strangled gargle, then the screaming stopped.

Silence again.

"You killed him!" Daphna raged at the Templar. "You killed my brother's soul!"

Before the Templar could respond, Daphna, hiding the barest trace of a smile, dove into the hole after her dead brother.

The Templars all hollered at Daphna to stop, but it was useless. She was sliding blindly down the stone incline, already wondering where Dexter was. She didn't have to wonder long. He cried out when she collided with him on the ledge he'd found, and then the two of them were sliding together.

The slope was perfectly smooth. It narrowed and then began to twist and turn, whipping the twins round bends and up and down roller coaster rises and drop-offs. Daphna managed to get hold of Dex, and then to wrap her wings around them both. The wings took the brunt of the bashing they received whipping around the sharper turns and past unforgiving bulges on the walls. Cocooned this way, the twins spiraled together down into the depths of the Well of Souls..

But then, finally, they fell onto solid ground.

Daphna's wings burst open, and Dex rolled out of them. Neither twin was hurt. Neither knew where they were, though. The sounds of outraged Templars was just the faintest echo coming down from above.

It was nearly pitch black.

Dex sat up and bumped his back into something hard. He reached for it. It felt like—a leg? For a moment he panicked, but then the leg fell over. It was stone, part of a statue.

Daphna was sitting up now, too.

"Can you see?" Dex asked.

"A bit," Daphna said, looking around. What she saw was odd and chilling. "We're in a cave. It's full of heads, arms, legs and torsos made out of stone. They're lying all over the place. It's like someone used this place to bury an army of dead statues, or a whole population of people hiding down here got petrified and fell apart."

"Weird. Are there any passageways or doors?"

"Doesn't look like it. I think this is really more of a giant hole."

"A well."

"What are we going to do now?" Daphna asked. "Eventually, they're going to figure out they can come down, though I guess I could just fly us over them if they do. But this cave isn't that high, and they'll probably leave some guys—"

An explosion cut Daphna off. It shook the entire cave, sending dirt and rubble cascading down from above. Then the twins heard gunfire, then shouting. And then it was quiet.

"What's going on?" Daphna whispered.

"Maybe someone saw us enter the fountain," Dex whispered. "We have to hurry!"

"How? What should we do? We're not actually looking for a stone, right?"

"Maybe it's down here, anyway—the Book of Letters, I mean—hidden in a stone. Set in a stone."

"Everything down here is stone!" Daphna hissed. There didn't seem to be a single statue in one piece, and the cavern was quite a bit bigger than she'd thought it was at first. "We can't search ten thousand broken statues!"

"Then there has to be more to the hint. If that's what it is."

"What exactly did the Secret Keeper say?"

"He said according to the fragment, the Grail was set in stone in King Solomon's Temple."

"Okay, okay," Daphna said, trying to calm down so she could think. "That has to have the hint in it. Oh, no! What if we have to translate all the letters into numbers—to find longitude and latitude coordinates—like how we found the Aleph?"

"But the Secret Keeper already told us it wasn't written in Hebrew," Dex pointed out. "He said it's in English, because Joseph—the guy who pretended to hide the Grail after Jesus died—he went to England."

"Right!"

Something metal clattering down the slope made the twins jump to their feet. It hit the ground not far from where they were standing.

A sword.

"Whoever's up there now is testing it out," Daphna realized. "We don't have much time! What else could 'set in stone' mean?"

Dex turned the phrase over in his mind. He wasn't up to this right now, stranded in the dark in the Well of Souls. How his life had brought him to this point was incomprehensible. "I don't know, Daphna," he admitted. "All I can think is that 'stone' must not mean stone—or not exactly stone, or not only stone—or there'd be no way to know which one it was down here."

"So what does it mean?"

"I don't know, Daphna! I'm last person in the world you want solving word puzzles for you!"

"Wait!" Daphna was watching the slope. So far, nothing but the sword had come down, but now she turned toward her brother. "Maybe the letters are a puzzle!" she suggested. "Maybe they're mixed up! Like an anagram!"

Dex sat back down and began massaging his eyebrows. He was getting a serious headache. He couldn't spell to save his life. He almost laughed at the thought that this might turn out to be literally true.

"Is 'stone' an anagram?" Daphna asked, scanning the room again.

"I don't know, Daphna," Dex groaned, massaging his forehead now.

"You can make the word 'notes' from the same letters. Does that help?"

"Maybe there are notes hidden around here with hints to the actual hiding spot," Dex tried, but with no hope in his voice.

"'Tones' is another one," Daphna realized. "Hey! Notes and tones both have to do with music! Is there anything to do with music down here?"

"That seems highly unlikely," Dex sighed, pressing

his thumbs just above his nose. A physical confrontation was coming and he was trying to prepare himself for it.

"Maybe we have to hum some frequency to open a secret door."

"But that has nothing to do with English, or any other language," Dex pointed out.

"But we're close, Dex!" Daphna insisted. *"English words may not have numbers, but they do often have more than one meaning."* With her brain whirring, for a moment she'd almost forgotten where she was and what danger they were in.

This was all crushing Dexter's brain. He massaged his forehead now, then moved his thumbs over his brows toward his ears and onto his...temples.

He looked up, eyes burst wide.

A second later the sound of someone sliding down to the Well echoed around them. A man cried out something in a language that wasn't English.

He was trying to stop sliding by scrabbling against the ramp walls, but he was failing.

There was suddenly light, and then it was bouncing on the floor.

A flashlight.

Dex leapt to pick it up. Moments later, legs shot into view from the hole in the cave wall. But the legs stopped before their owner appeared.

The man cried out again, some other word. And just like that his legs disappeared.

"He's on a rope!" Daphna realized. "They're going to see he's okay and all come down!" She leapt to rush up the slope to grab the man, but her brother grabbed her instead.

"Forget him!" Dex cried. "I know where the Grail is!"

CHAPTER THIRTY-THREE
The Temple of King Solomon

"What? The Book of Letters? Where?"

The end of six ropes tied to Templar helmets suddenly fell out of the hole in the wall.

"Start looking for a head," Dex whispered, waving the light over the field of what looked like mostly rubble. *"A head with a crown." All this junk is just—* cover."

"What are you talking about?"

Shouting now came from above. Lots of shouting. It was the shouting, the twins could tell, of instructions.

They were coming down.

"It's it King Solomon's head!" Dex shouted. "In his *temple!"*

Daphna looked at the intensity in her brother's speckled eyes and swallowed any further protest. She spun round and ran further into the Well. Dex did the same, waving the flashlight around as he went.

It was difficult to make progress because broken arms and legs were everywhere. Daphna stepped over them as best she could, but in many places there was hardly room to put her foot down. There were plenty of heads, but none that she could see with a crown. She ran around, taking random paths through what seemed like acres of clutter, flicking her powerful eyes from one piece of rubble to the next.

Dex was running around too, in equally random directions, whipping the light from cracked torsos to hands with missing fingers to feet with broken toes. He saw the occasional blank, noseless face, but nothing like a head with a crown. He tripped and fell, got up, tripped and fell again, and again, got up.

"There!" someone shouted.

Dex froze.

Lights were on him.

He switched his light off and dropped to the ground, then crawled to another spot.

Daphna did not do likewise. She'd seen the men enter the cave, but instead of hiding, she stayed where she was, looking at them—or at one of them. They were looking at her now too, standing with their backs against the wall they'd come through, playing their lights over her face and wings. They said nothing at the sight of her, but Daphna could sense their awe. There were six men. Five were in olive military uniforms, just like those worn by the men fighting on the Mount, though these all had Hebrew writing on them.

The sixth man was clearly not a soldier of any kind, and it was he who held Daphna's attention.

He was tall with a well-trimmed white beard falling a few inches below his chin. A white turban sat atop his head, which might or might not have been attached to the gold headband encircling his forehead. He seemed to be robed in layers. The bottom of a white robe was revealed above his feet and wrists, but overtop that was a stunning, bright blue robe—the word 'topaz' came to Daphna's mind. On top of that was something like an apron—a tunic?—embroidered with purple and blue and scarlet and gold. It was bound by a sash of the same colors. Over *that,* the man wore a breastplate inset with multi-colored precious stones.

Then Daphna saw the man's eyes. They were eyes that did not look upon this world, she was sure. She was certain they looked beyond it.

"He's a Kohen Gadol—a high priest," Dexter said from somewhere in the dark. "He's here to read the Name in the Holy of Holies." Dex had only gotten the quickest and dimmest look at the man, but he's seen enough to put two and two together.

Daphna knew he was right.

"Have you found the book?" one of the soldiers asked. He spoke English with a heavy Israeli accent.

"You've always known what was going on down here—about the Templars—haven't you?" Daphna asked.

"Of course!" the soldier replied. "How could the Israeli government not know? A delicate balance we have maintained allowing all the others to think it was under their control. They wait? We have waited."

Dex tried to formulate a plan while he hid among

the shattered statue parts, but he just couldn't think. Daphna needed to stall. He leaned back to release tension in his spine but was jabbed by something sharp. His hand went back to feel for the culprit.

"But the Cone—the High Priests," Daphna said, "they've been dead for centuries."

"So the world believes," the same soldier said. He seemed to be in charge of this new group. "You are testing us," he decided, as everyone faced with a Wax angel's ignorance had. "Of course we have not failed to protect and prepare them through every generation as we are waiting for this day."

Dex found the culprit. A pointed stone. His hand moved down alongside it and found another point rising up right next to it. He turned around to examine it more closely.

"You have come to retrieve the Book of Letters for us," the soldier continued. Daphna realized as he spoke that none of the men had moved even the slightest bit away from the wall, and that the High Priest seemed to have no intention of speaking. "Do you have it now?" the soldier asked.

"Um," Daphna said.

Dexter got to his knees and used both hands to feel the spikes. There were many moving around the top of—yes—a head, a very large head.

It was a crown.

"Don't tell them anything!" Dex shouted. Lights suddenly flicked in his direction. "They can't move around down here and risk stepping into the Holy of Holies—even the High Priest because it's not the right day."

Daphna didn't know what to do.

Dexter's hands ran frantically over the statue's face and head.

"There is no time," the soldier insisted, though calmly. "We will send this Devil back to Hell. You and your brother may be free to tread here, but only we can do such a thing. Only the Kohen Gadol can pronounce the Name."

"I—" Daphna stuttered, "I—I don't know what to do. I need a moment to think what's best." This was, anyway, the simple truth.

"Yes!" Dex agreed. "Take a moment to think! Take two!" The nose was chipped, but mostly there.

With shaking hands, he pressed his thumbs into the eyes, then slowly slid them around toward the back of the head.

"After you say the Name and send the Devil back," Daphna asked, wondering what her brother was doing, willing him to do—something. She was staring at the High Priest's eyes, wondering what they saw, wondering if they saw hers in the darkness. "What will you do with the Book of Letters?"

"We will ensure that God's law is the law of the land—of all lands."

"And how will you do that, exactly?"

"By summoning the wrath of God and unleashing it on all who disobey."

"Dexter," Daphna said, suddenly having her answer. "We're not giving these people the Grail."

Dex's thumbs found their way into slight depressions between the statue's eyes and ears—into its *temples*. Immediately, his right thumb sank into the stone.

"They're no different from the Secret Keeper and his kind."

There was a small, but audible *click,* and then the entire head simply fell apart in Dexter's hands. "I found it!" he involuntarily cried.

In his hands was now a book, a golden book with a key sticking into the center of its cover. Both the book and key glowed brightly.

Daphna turned toward the light suddenly illuminating the cave and saw her brother standing there with the Holy Grail in his hands.

Dex stared at the shining book, dumbfounded. "Temple," he said, mostly to himself. "King Solomon's *temple*." His skin felt electrified. His heart was beating so hard he feared it would explode.

"Bring me the Book of Letters," someone said.

Daphna turned away from her brother toward the voice, which sounded odd, almost elfish. It was the High Priest who'd spoken, and he was pointing at Dex. The soldiers did not move. They'd still not moved an inch.

"Show me the Holy of Holies," the High Priest commanded. "Bring me the book so that on Yom Kippur, I may set the world to rights."

Daphna looked at her brother again. He was still

staring at the book, shaking all over.

"Dex," she tried, but he did not respond.

"The book, my angel," the High Priest said, softly now. "Bring me the book."

"Sorry to disappoint you," Dex said, finally looking up. "But we have dibs."

At this, the Kohen Gadol turned to the soldiers and nodded.

Guns were aimed at Dexter.

Daphna streaked across the cave.

Triggers were pulled.

Bullets flew.

But Daphna reached her brother first.

She wrapped herself around Dex, shielding him from the onslaught with her wings.

The bullets struck.

Daphna cried out.

Dexter's body was hot to the touch, and his skin was shining just like the book in his hands. Holding him, Daphna knew that whatever was happening to him was starting to happen to her, too.

The bullets continued to fly, but Daphna no longer felt their bite. All was quiet under the shelter of her wings. She reached out and put her hands on the Book of Letters next to her twin's.

Dexter and Daphna understood the Grail's immeasurable power. They could feel it in their blood and bones.

In one voice, they spoke one awful word: "Hellmouth."

And then they were gone.

CHAPTER THIRTY-FOUR
Stretched

It was just a moment, but it stretched.

Daphna was cast into an inky darkness. Her body was still, but somehow also traveling an unfathomable speed: she was pure thought, streaming through the void.

Quinn! her mind called out. *We got it! We got the Grail!*

She strained to hear his voice.

I'm afraid! Daphna told him. *How will we make him destroy the very thing he seeks? I need your help!*

Daphna listened, but heard no reply.

And that was good.

Dex felt atomized, that his atoms had burst across the universe all at once. He felt speed, astonishing speed, but also stillness at his core. He saw nothing, yet it all rushed past in a mind-numbing whirl.

Dex!

"Nora?"

Dex, please! Please hurry. My time is running out.

We've got the Book, Nora! We found it! I'm coming to get you!

I knew you would, Dex! I knew you would! Hurry! I love you! I love you!

Dex felt he was becoming himself again. Nora's voice was fading, but before it was gone, she said one more thing. And despite how faint it was, Dexter heard her loud and clear:

Don't let her stop you.

I won't, Dex promised. *I won't.*

CHAPTER THIRTY-FIVE
Already Too Late

It was still dark, but there was substance to the darkness now. Gradually, it resolved itself into smoke, the filthy, fetid, mustard-colored smoke with which the twins were unfortunately already familiar. It was rising up all around the them, enveloping them completely for long, suffocating stretches, then letting them loose according to the whims of the winds whipping round. For brief moments the twins could see each other's frightened, disoriented faces.

At some point, Dex and Daphna realized they were both still clutching the Grail.

Two sets of hands tugged on it in two different directions.

Daphna let go.

A powerful gust swept by, momentarily clearing the choking spumes, giving the twins a glimpse of their surroundings.

It seemed at first that they were in some kind of cage because bar-like shapes were curving down over them, though on second thought the shapes looked more like fingers, or the claws of some monster about to crush their bones. But now Dex and Daphna could see that they were roots, giant roots—the roots of a great tree that had barely managed to avoid plummeting into the pit. They were on a ledge just below the lip of the crater, under the tree.

On their tiptoes, the twins found they could see through the tangle of roots out and over the lip.

"No lights," Daphna whispered. "Where is every-one?" It was dark up there. Scary dark.

"Listen," Dex said. He was looking up.

Daphna heard it now too. Sounds from above.

Planes.

Dexter met his sister's eyes for a moment, then put the Grail, whatever it actually was, into her hands. Then he reached up under the tree trunk for a leaf, hoping it was what it looked like. When Dex brought it down, he had to squint to see it in his palm, but it was what he thought it was, a little helicopter leaf-pod.

It was the ash tree, *his* ash tree, in his Clearing. This was all that was left of it.

Dex suddenly remembered collapsing in the Clearing after he'd been choked and humiliated by Asterius Rash's brainwashed bully of an assistant, Emmet. It was just as this endless nightmare was first taking shape around him. He'd wished there was a pit there he could jump into.

Dex turned to his sister to say something about being careful what you wished for, but she was no longer standing there.

She was in a heap at his feet.

All Dex could see were Daphna's voluminous wings—the wings he'd assumed would take them down quickly and easily into this infernal pit. But now he saw that the great ivory feathers were streaked with blood.

She'd been shot! He'd somehow already forgotten. Dex helped his sister onto her side.

"I'm—I'm losing them," she moaned.

"Does it hurt?"

"Take them. They're letting go."

Dex wasn't exactly sure what he needed to do, but he put his hands under the wings as gently as he could, then carefully began to lift. They were incredibly heavy. It was like lifting a live animal. But he kept lifting as carefully as he could, waiting for his sister to cry out. She didn't though, and suddenly he was standing above her with the wings in his hands.

"Daphna?"

She was crying, but her back didn't appear to be bleeding. It seemed the nerves didn't rip out of her skin. It was difficult to see through the smoke, but it appeared they'd simply pulled free like hair from a scalp. He caught sight of little raised bumps through the slits in her shirt, but they seemed already to be receding.

"Just let me breathe a minute," Daphna whispered. *"I need oxygen."*

Dex didn't know what to do with the wings. He couldn't imagine leaving them on this ledge, but Daphna had just given him an idea. He turned and lifted them over the lip of the crater. A book—the library book—fell out as he tucked them among the roots of the ash tree. Then he turned back to his sister, who was sobbing silently.

"My wings," Daphna choked. "My *wings*."

"I lost mine too, Daphna."

Daphna jerked upright. *"What was that?"* She'd heard something, not from above—from somewhere nearby in the smoke.

Dex hadn't heard anything, but he looked the way Daphna was looking, which was into the haze where the ledge sloped into the crater. They could see now that it was the path that wound down into the darkness along the pit's wall.

The path. They were at the top of it.

"Who's there?" Daphna shouted, scrambling to her feet.

This time, Dex heard the noise, too. A shuffling sound. He snatched the Grail off the ground where Daphna had dropped it. She snatched up the library book and held it out defensively.

The twins looked at each other, then back into the darkness along the ledge.

"I'm not ready for this," Daphna hissed. "We have no plan!"

"Shhh!"

"Can we climb out?" Daphna looked desperately up at the roots of the ash tree.

"Shhh!" Dex strained his ears. If someone was there, what was the point of running away? Why had they come, after all? Dex looked down at the Grail. It was emanating a soft light.

It would defend them.

Dexter edged forward a bit down along the ledge, peering into the smoke.

"Dex!" Daphna warned, backing up against the crater wall. She turned, reached up for a root, and used it to help her rise on her toes enough to see over the lip again. Yes, she could use it to pull herself up. "Dex!" she repeated, turning back now to insist they get out of there before it was too late.

But it was already too late. Her brother was gone.

CHAPTER THIRTY-SIX
Over the Edge

"Dexter!" Daphna screamed. When she heard no reply, she rushed blindly into the smoke. But after no more than five steps, she crashed right into him, knocking them both down. Falling in a tangle, she panicked further, fearing she'd send them right over the ledge and into the abyss.

When that didn't happen, Daphna lost it. This was the last straw. "Stop it!" she screamed. "Just stop it! Stop going off without even—! It's because you aren't breathing! You aren't even trying to control your—!"

At that moment, someone stumbling up the ledge tripped over the twins and went sprawling. The body landed beyond them with a thud, after which came a strangled gasp and a long, weak, rather high-pitched groan.

The twins froze in their tangle for a moment, listening, bracing for a struggle or, more likely, a fight in the dark. But the body was silent now, and it wasn't moving.

Dexter shoved his sister off him, and they both got to their feet. Daphna reached out for Dexter's arm when he took a step toward the prone figure, but he shook her off. She saw their two books at her feet, so she quickly shoved the Grail under her shirt and picked up the library book.

The smoke cleared a moment, then swept back in.

"It's Picker," Dex said, kneeling next to the body. "I think he's dead."

"What?" Daphna was both relieved and concerned. She moved up next to Dex and saw that it was, in fact, Picker. She knelt down too, and when the smoke cleared again for a moment, she winced at what had become of the poor man. He was just as frail and emaciated as he'd appeared on the video after coming out of his coma, but now his hospital gown was in bloody tatters. He looked like he'd been attacked by a wild animal. His face was scratched and bleeding, and his hair seemed to have been ripped out in chunks off his head.

"Famous," Picker moaned. *"Famous."*

"He's alive!" Daphna cried. "Picker?"

Picker's eyes, now open but glassy, suddenly focused. They shot back and forth between the twins. "You!" he cried.

"Yes, Picker—*Arthur,* I mean," Daphna said. "It's us again." She set down the library book and took his limp hands into hers.

"There's still time!" Picker croaked, turning his head weakly to see his hand in Daphna's. He appeared to want to get up, but couldn't manage it.

Here they were again.

"What happened to you?" Daphna asked.

"Why do you want to be famous so badly, anyway?" Dex wanted to know.

The little man's eyes turned to Dexter, fervent in the foul smoke.

"Fame makes you real," he said, rather clearly now. "Fame is wealth. Fame is power." His voice rose quickly to a fever pitch. "Fame is everything! Fame is forever! *Fame! Is! Heaven!"*

Dex did not reply to this. He didn't know what kind of answer he'd been expecting, but it hadn't been that.

Daphna was a bit stunned too, so she didn't react when Picker suddenly sat up, grabbed her library book, and clambered to his feet.

Before either twin could think to do anything, he screamed, "PICKER GOT THE GRAIL! HE GOT IT FOR YOU!"

And then he took a flying leap right off the edge of the path.

Stunned, the twins got to their feet and peered into the pit. Daphna reached out uselessly for the little man, but he was long gone, a black shadow falling through the rising smoke, screaming in triumph. They heard the cry of *"Faaaaamous!"* echoing up through the crater long after the last sign of him had vanished. Finally, there came a soft thud that sent a shiver down both their spines.

"He took the wrong book," Daphna said, taking the Grail out. She was incredibly glad, of course, but also terribly sad.

"He took the library book!" Dex raged, finally processing what had happened. "That was our only connection to Nora! Why didn't you read it yet?"

"What? I—I—"

"I'll tell you why! Because you've known all along that Quinn was probably okay, and YOU DON'T GIVE A DAMN ABOUT NORA!"

"That's not true," Daphna said, shocked by Dex's sudden fury. She didn't yell back, though. In fact, her response came out as not much more than a whisper: "I swear to God that's not true." But she was thinking, Could it be true? No—

Dex, surprised by Daphna's failure to attack back, didn't know what to say or do next.

"Breathe, Dex. Please. Just breathe."

Dexter tried. He looked down at the Grail in his sister's hand and sucked the heinous smoke into his throat.

"I'm sorry, Dex," Daphna said, "but there just hasn't been enough time. We should count ourselves lucky he took the wrong book because this is the one that's going to bring Nora back. It's going to fix everything for everyone," she promised. "Here, you carry it."

Dex took the Grail. He breathed. Then he closed his eyes and squeezed the awesome book with all his might. He wished with every fiber of his being that Nora were there, standing right beside him.

Nothing happened.

"Sorry," Daphna said again. This time because it was obvious what her brother was doing

Dex opened his eyes. "Why don't we just use this to transport ourselves down to the bottom?" he said, refusing to accept his sister's sympathy.

Daphna considered the suggestion for a moment, but then shook her head. "We tried that at Eden," she said. "Remember? It was a trap. And besides, it took us here from the Well of Souls, not down there. I think it might be best to go it on our own from here."

"Okay. You're probably right."

"Dex," Daphna added, "since we're doing this.

We—we can't forget—our ribs. If anything happens—"

"One of us has to live."

Daphna nodded. "Let's just get going," she said, relieved to have dodged disaster between them, if only for the moment. "At least we have plenty of time."

"It didn't sound like Picker thought so."

"That's true," Daphna admitted, concerned. "He seemed to think there was hardly any."

"Well, you *are* cutting it a bit close, don't you think?" someone said, a shadow walking slowly up the path from the smoky depths.

In one hand the shadow was holding a powerful flashlight, powerful enough to illuminate its other hand.

Which held a gun.

Daphna didn't bother with the breathing, nor did her brother. All they could muster was two bone-weary sighs. They knew well before the figure got close enough to see that it was Branwen.

CHAPTER THIRTY-SEVEN
Idiots

They almost didn't recognize her. Branwen had somehow become, or re-become, *Branwen*. Even in the dim, smoky light, it was clear that her famous raven tresses had been restored to their former glory, even if they looked slightly frayed and flyaway. Her face was bruise- and blemish-free, if a bit pale, and her teeth gleamed like little beacons. She was wearing expensive hiking gear, including a helmet, red storm jacket, and thick-soled boots. A high-tech daypack was slung over her shoulder.

Despite themselves, both Dex and Daphna thought she was beautiful.

Branwen seemed to revel in the thoughts she knew she was provoking in the twins, but then the glimmer of satisfaction passed, and she looked only royally pissed. "You two clearly have a flair for the dramatic," she sneered, "but this is a bit much, don't you think? I've been waiting here for days! You might have at least taken a shower and put on some clean clothes, don't you think?"

Daphna, as baffled by this bizarre apparition as her brother, gestured behind Branwen. There was a tent pitched back where the crater wall angled a bit over a deep recess. The twins looked at each other, then warily back at Branwen, wondering how it was possible for her to appear here, now, and this way—and what she was playing at.

"You don't even know," Branwen concluded. "Great. Perfect."

"Branwen," Daphna said, trying hard to process this new, sudden, and disorienting situation, "what are you—?"

"*That holiday*," Branwen sighed. She looked at her watch, which glowed indigo when she pressed a button. "It starts at sundown tonight, at 7:23—*Hello?*"

"*Tonight?*" The twins went white.

"That's in four hours, you idiots!"

"We lost time!" Daphna cried. They'd lost time using the Aleph as a portal, and now the same had happened with the Grail. Neither twin could believe they hadn't considered the possibility before risking—everything! But of course there hadn't been time to think.

"Four hours?" Dex was beside himself. "Four hours?"

"Take this," Branwen said, digging into her pack. She pulled out a watch and tossed it to Daphna. "I have an extra, and I don't want you screwing this up any worse."

Daphna had no idea what Branwen was talking about, but she was grateful for the watch, which she quickly strapped on. Then she navigated to the stopwatch to start a countdown.

"Let's go!" Dex shouted. "Let's go!" But then he said, "I'm starving." He wasn't nearly as drained as he'd been after passing through the Light, but the weakness he felt was significant. Fatigue was radiating through his arms and legs.

"Me, too," Daphna realized, suddenly aware of how depleted she felt as well. But what did that matter? They had four hours to save Nora and Dr. Fludd and Quinn's folks. Four hours!

"Too bad I'm out of food," Branwen said, oblivious of or unconcerned with the twins' problems. "Do you have any idea how unpleasant it's been down—Anyway," she interrupted herself, "is that it?" She pointed at the softly glowing book with its protruding key still in Dexter's hand. "It that what all the fuss is about?"

"Yes," Dex quickly confirmed. Then he simply handed it to Branwen.

Daphna looked at him like he'd lost his mind, but as Branwen examined the luminous covers and fingered the key, Dex said, "It has a kind of magic word in it. A mystical word. You can open the book with that key. Whoever reads the word can pretty much make anything happen. Anything in the world."

"I should shoot you right now," Branwen spat, raising the gun to Dexter's face. "I heard everything in the truck," she said, "and I heard everything in that operating room. I made the stupid doctor tell me everything he knows, too. It's obvious no one knows exactly what the hell this is. But I think I'll pass on killing my own soul for now." She took several steps back and stuffed the book into her pack. Then she took a second flashlight out and tossed it to Dexter, who barely managed to catch it.

"What do you want, Branwen?" Daphna asked.

"I WANT WREN! AND I WANT MY LIFE BACK!"

Branwen's voice echoed through the pit like the cry of some tortured animal. She took a long, deep breath to calm herself—something not unlike the type of breaths the twins had been practicing—then said, "Now *move*." She waved the gun so Dex and Daphna would walk in front of her. "Stay along the wall," she ordered, "the ledge gets narrow in places."

Dex turned on the flashlight, which was incredibly powerful for its size. Even so, most of the illumination it produced was swallowed up by the rising vapors. Pointing it at the ground helped a bit.

"I said move!"

The twins did as they were told, both trying to forget how hungry they were. They remembered the first of many times they'd been forced at gunpoint to walk toward their likely deaths. It was quite possible that they were walking the very same path right now, just a few dozen or so feet below it. It seemed like they'd been walking the same path all their lives, or that all the paths they'd ever taken had always been leading to the same place: The End.

CHAPTER THIRTY-EIGHT
The Archway

"We couldn't use it anyway," Dex whispered. *"Time."*

Daphna looked at him. It took a moment, but then she realized what he meant: Using the book to get away from Branwen might cost them the last few hours they had.

"Shut up," Branwen said.

So the twins walked slowly and silently into the stinking smoke, keeping their shoulders in contact with the crater wall. The surface of the ledge was full of rocks and uneven ridges, all of which seemed poised to send them hurtling over the edge like Picker.

Picker.

The absurd little man's obsession with being famous struck Dex as ridiculous at first, but he felt implicated by his last words. Hadn't he been craving something similar for so long now? Why did he need to be praised so much? Hadn't he positively basked in the adulation he'd received as an angel? *But, Dex thought, Picker wanted to be famous for nothing. I don't need people to remember me forever. I just want them to recognize me for all I've actually accomplished. Does God know what I've accomplished, wherever he is? Does it make a difference?*

Dex swept the light back and forth across the ledge as he walked and thought, making sure to mark where it dropped off every step of the way. Branwen was right about it getting rather narrow at points. She was walking silently behind the twins, but broadcasting her hatred for them loud and clear.

Daphna pulled her collar up over her nose to filter the stench, and she kept one hand on her brother's back as she made her fearful way behind him. She was thinking about Picker, too. Who was he really? Just a guy who wanted to be loved—no different than anyone else.

No different from her.

She remembered being told how Wren had salvaged the Pops' dignity after Daphna turned the tables on their little attempt to dump a bucket of cleanser on her—Wren told everyone that Pops were Pops only because everyone thought they were Pops. In other words, everyone loved them because—Well, because they were loved. Or something circular and stupid but real like that. It boiled down to the fact that perception made reality. *Was that what Picker was saying about fame? If you believe in God,* she wondered, *does that make him exist? If you don't believe in God, does that mean he doesn't?*

The path descended sharply, and it became and stayed very narrow, so now the twins had to guard even closer against falling. Both put Picker out of their minds, as neither could spare another thought for anything other than avoiding plummeting to their deaths—or to worse.

They moved slowly. The only good thing was that it wasn't particularly hot, certainly not as hot as it was on the surface. If anything, it was getting cooler.

Dex stopped. "Umm," he said, shining his light at what appeared to be a dead end. There was a shrouded wall blocking the path ahead. "Now what?" he asked. "Wait—are these bricks?" There seemed to be an arch set into a wall of earth.

Branwen stepped forward and added her light to what Dex was trying to illuminate. "Not exactly," she said.

Daphna stepped forward, peering into the smoke as Dex and Branwen swept their lights around, trying to penetrate the sickening puffs and tendrils swirling about. "It's an archway," she said, putting her hands on what had looked to her like bricks as well. "But these aren't bricks."

"They're books," said Branwen.

And now the twins could see that she was right. The arch was at least twenty feet high, and it was made of books, four layers of books jammed together into the dirt at odd angles.

But there was no way through it.

"I couldn't find any kind of door," Branwen said. "And I wasn't about to dig for one."

"But there must be a door," Daphna assumed. "Picker must have come through. But maybe it's easier from the other side."

"It can't be that hard," Dex promised, swishing his light around. "The Dragon asked for someone to bring him the book."

"Well," Daphna said, "what should we do?"

"We just have the find a handle or something. But I can't see well enough."

Branwen stepped closer with her light, but then stopped and jumped back when the wall of earth under the arch seemed to shake.

It stopped.

"What's going on?" Daphna asked, fearing a quake.

Dex thought a minute, then said, "I was right."

"What do you mean?"

"He asked someone to bring him the book." Dex turned to Branwen and said, "Move close again."

Branwen hesitated for a moment, then took a small step toward the archway. The earth below it trembled again. She moved even closer.

A door began to open in the wall.

When it had opened completely, Dex, Daphna, and Branwen found themselves staring into more smoke and darkness behind it.

"Go," Branwen ordered.

Daphna turned to her and said, "We want the same thing you do, you know—to get back the people we've lost."

"I don't care about the people you've lost," Branwen retorted. "Why would I care about the people you've lost?"

"Because we're all in the same boat, here, Branwen. We need to work together to figure out how to set things right."

"Good luck with that."

Daphna turned back to Dex and said, "She wants to trade the Book for Wren and Teal." Then, to Branwen, she said, "You do realize Teal is actually dead, though, right? As in *dead*, dead, from the plague?" She was immediately sorry to have brought that up. The look on Branwen's face was positively murderous.

Dexter stepped in. "What do you need us for, anyway?" he asked. "That *thing* could be right through that arch waiting for you. No, wait," he reconsidered. "If he was in there, Picker wouldn't have jumped. He must be at the bottom."

"Branwen," Daphna warned, cringing at her owns words even as she uttered them, "he's not going to *trade*. You can't be foolish enough to try that. He's just going to take the book, and then you'll be—"

"So what if it's foolish, you stupid rejects!" Branwen railed. "We're all dead, anyway!"

"What do you mean?"

"Jesus! Where have you been? You haven't seen the news, either?"

"What news?"

"Seeing three 'angels' flying around got everyone to stop killing each other," Branwen impatiently explained, "so the fighting stopped up there. But there's no arguing anymore about what's really going on, or what's down in this charming little hole. The whole world knows the Holy Grail has been found—though no one agrees what it really is. The whole freaking planet is holding its breath."

"And?" Dex said.

"*But*," Branwen corrected. "They're not about to put all their money on a couple of teenage angels."

"What do you mean?" Daphna asked. "Does this have something to do with why no one is out there around the rim?

"I heard a plane," Dex said. "A bunch of them."

"The rim?" Branwen laughed. "There's no one on the West Coast of the United States."

"*What?*" the twins both asked. "Why?"

"Because if anything climbs out of this stinking pit without a pair of wings on its back and a set of bloody horns in its hands, every country that can is going to drop a nuclear bomb into it. Or they're going to try, which will get them bombed back. Unless the US just does it itself, which people are saying is what they're secretly planning so they can blame it on someone else and start a war—the war to end all wars. So, like I said, we're all dead, anyway. So I'll just take my own chances, thank you very much."

"Super," Dex said, suddenly foreseeing the perfect ending to their story: save the world for the millionth time, and then get their just reward—nuclear bombs dropped on their heads.

"That must be what all the planes are," Daphna groaned, feeling faint.

"To answer your first question—" Branwen said, turning to Dex, "I need you to walk ahead of me in case there are traps or drop-offs. You two are my shields." She raised her gun again and added, "Now get through that door right now because I really only need one of you."

The twins each let out one more defeated sigh, then walked through the archway.

CHAPTER THIRTY-NINE
Perfect

"There's light," Branwen said after following the twins into—wherever they were now. It was a long, narrow hall channeled right into the earth. Torches in brackets at intervals along the earthen walls were casting flickering lights through the smoke.

"Perfect," two voices said when their eyes adjusted well enough to see what lined the walls.

The voices belonged to Dexter and Branwen.

They were in a library.

"I don't understand this," Branwen said, shining her light around. Shelves had been carved right into the earth, and they were full of books, frightening books with reptilian covers. They were packed awkwardly, willy-nilly it seemed, with some stacked lying flat next to others standing upright or jammed in diagonally. Most were rectangular, but there were others in all kinds of unexpected shapes: round, triangular—one was even a star. Covered in dirt and dust and crawling with spiders and insects, they all seemed to seethe with malice.

"What don't you understand?" Daphna asked.

"Books," Branwen said. "Why is everything about books!"

"Good question," Dex said. "A very, very good question."

"I despise books," Branwen ranted. "Books are for nerds. Books are for losers. Books are—"

"There's something seriously wrong with these books," Daphna whispered, trying to resist the urge to throttle Branwen. She was taking slow steps forward, peering closely at the evil-looking tomes, but fearful of touching any. She was as afraid of the bugs as the books, none of which had visible titles on their spines. She saw one tied with a rusty chain like some kind of dangerous animal.

"They reek," Branwen complained. It was true.

There was a smell coming off the books not entirely unlike the stench of the smoke. But it had more of an edge to it, like rotting meat. "Get going," she said after glancing at her watch. "We have barely more than three hours now."

Daphna looked at her watch to confirm this.

The trio began to walk quickly, following the corridor as it turned this way and that. They moved in a single file, all trying to avoid even brushing up against the books, some of which were more than just ominous. There was an open volume with mutilated pages hanging out of its covers like guts. Many seemed to be dripping some kind of sticky fluid. There was an entire shelf of books with nails sticking up through their covers. Another had books with large spikes driven down through them into the earth.

One huge book sitting alone on a shelf had something sticking out of it that looked very much like a claw.

As Daphna moved past the filthy, creepy books, she could swear they were somehow watching her.

"What's that sound?" Dex suddenly asked.

Everyone stopped to listen. There was a faint scratching sound, very faint, but very there.

"Just keep going," Branwen said from the back of the line.

So they kept going.

It seemed to Dex like the books were somehow sniffing the air as he passed. He saw one in the shadows of a shelf that he was pretty sure had an eye that blinked at him, and it made him think of the Eye—the all-seeing Eye he and Daphna had briefly glimpsed when they'd seen everything, all that was, in the Aleph. It had seemed afraid, but maybe it was his own fear Dex had seen. Why had he not thought about the Eye since then? *It was too much, that's why.*

"I swear to God these books are staring at me," Branwen complained.

"I need food," was Daphna's reply. "I need it soon, or I'm going to pass out."

"Shut up and keep going."

"Branwen—" Daphna started to scold. She was getting weaker by the minute. But she suddenly pulled up short. They'd reached a spot where the earthen corridor branched off in two directions.

"Anyone see a cookbook?" Dex said. He was in serious need of food, too. "I'm sure we can find a recipe for batwing soup or something."

"Look," Branwen said. She was shining her light into a shelf directly in front of them where there was what looked like a cluster of roots growing out of a dirt shelf in the wall.

"Is that a potato?" Daphna asked. There appeared to be a small, misshapen potato attached to the roots.

Dex stepped closer and shone the light on the roots. He saw that they ran along the shelf a bit, so he tracked them with the light until—

"It's growing out of that book," Daphna said. There was a book lying flat on the shelf. The roots traveled right into it, disappearing under its cover.

"Open it," Branwen ordered, but neither twin stepped forward to comply. "Open it!"

"I really don't think that's a good idea," Daphna warned.

"Oh, for crying out loud," Branwen sighed. "You've been whining like babies for—" She opened the book while she spoke, and now, looking into it, said, "There's nothing inside."

It appeared she was right. There were no pages in the book, just an empty cover sitting on the dirt. The roots trailed right down through the back cover into the ground.

Branwen grabbed them and pulled.

Out popped a dozen more ugly, misshapen potatoes. "See," she said, "it's just—"

Branwen screamed.

The roots were wrapping themselves around her wrist and pulling her hand toward the book.

"Help!" she screamed, trying to pull away. "Get it off! Get it off!"

The twins rushed to the shelf and looked with horror into the book. The dirt inside was loose now and draining into a deep hole. Not a hole, they now saw—a mouth, a mouth full of teeth.

"Help!" Branwen had fallen to the ground and was trying to prevent herself from being yanked back to her feet, but her arm was over her head and being pulled out of its socket. Daphna grabbed the arm and tried to use it to pull the roots further out of the book, but to little effect. The roots were now wrapped around Branwen's stomach. "My bag!" Branwen wailed. "Knife!"

The bag was on the ground, so Dex grabbed it, ripped the zipper open, then dumped its contents out. A silver knife caught his eye.

"Dex!" Daphna cried. She had her arms wrapped around Branwen's waist. Branwen's arm, head, and left shoulder were now in the dirt mouth. They couldn't even hear her screaming any more. She kicked wildly, which was making it hard for Daphna to hold on to her.

Dex got his fingers under a strand of roots around Branwen's waist, but held the knife back.

"Dex!" Daphna screamed again. "What are you doing?"

"Let her go."

"What? But—" Daphna had acted out of instinct, but now—

She looked at Dex, who looked at her back.

"Let her go, Daphna," he said. "We did this once already, and it was a mistake. This is our chance." Dex took several large steps back.

Branwen continued to kick and flail. Daphna was losing her.

Dexter had the Grail. He was walking away.

Daphna looked down at what else Dex had dumped on the ground.

The gun was there.

Daphna let go for just a moment and grabbed it, then leapt back onto Branwen's calves, which where were now all that was sticking out of the shelf. She jammed the gun under Branwen's body and pulled the trigger. Then she pulled it again. And again and again until it wouldn't fire any more.

Branwen stopped struggling. Her body went limp.

Daphna despaired, but then the roots went lax.

Branwen's feet began to kick again, and Daphna could somehow sense they were telling her they expected to be saved.

Hating the girl with every fiber of her being, Daphna dragged her out of the earth.

CHAPTER FORTY
The Little Black Dress

Branwen was covered in dirt from her head to her ankles. It was all over her face and caked in her hair. Sitting with her head between her knees, she coughed clumps of it out. When she was done, without even acknowledging Daphna, she began sorting through the strewn contents of her bag.

Daphna saw what most of it was now: beauty supplies. There were bags and bags of them. And a battery-operated curling iron. Branwen found some wipes and began washing her face with one.

Dex was there again. Daphna let out a sigh of relief.

"Why?" Branwen asked, working the wipe over her neck. "Last time it was you who wanted me dead. Why'd you bother? The only reason I haven't killed you both is that I need you right now."

"I don't know," Daphna muttered. "Maybe because I used to be an angel. But probably because I'll never learn."

"We always hated you."

"What?" Daphna cried, now furious. "What did I ever do to you? Any of you!"

"You *were* an angel," Branwen said. "You were *always* the angel. You might think everyone's worshipping you up there—" She pointed up to the surface of the Earth. "But that's because they're afraid. People *hate* angels."

"What are you talking about?"

Branwen kept wiping herself down. "You were always so perfect," she spat, "like you were above the concerns the rest of us ordinary humans had to deal with. But you were really no different than anyone else. That's half the reason we picked you to cheat off of—to teach *you* a lesson. You think you were the only smart kid who would give Pops their work? *Please.*"

Daphna, flummoxed to be suddenly having this conversation—How could she be having this conversation, here? Now? Despite how inappropriate it was, how ridiculous and wrong it was, she was reeling. "But you—you—" she stammered, "you and Teal and Wren—you—"

"I know you think we were a bunch of stuck up bitches."

"Only because you were," Dex said.

"Shut up!" Branwen shouted at him. Her face and neck were clean, so she started working on her arms. "You don't know anything about our lives," she snapped at Daphna. "You played the misunderstood loner, and I'm sure it got you whatever twisted life you wanted out of it. Wren's sister made her clean for her, cook for her, wash her clothes. And if she wouldn't, she'd ruin her life in a thousand little ways no one could pin on her."

Daphna nodded.

"Interesting, huh? Did you know Teal was on antidepressants since she was ten?"

Dex was sorry he'd said anything, even though it actually felt sort of daring to have done so. He'd never actually had a conversation with a Pop girl in his entire life. "Nice," he said, spotting a bunch of protein bars that had fallen out of Branwen's pack. "Ran out of food, eh?" He picked two up and tossed one to Daphna.

Daphna tore into it without comment. *So what?* was her internal response to Branwen's news. People weren't what they seemed. Life was hard for everyone. This was not news. What mattered was how you acted.

"And what was *your* big secret problem?" Dex asked Branwen, picking up a bag of some kind of girl junk. He couldn't help butting back in, which amazed him a bit. *Who didn't have a big secret problem?* "The agony of never finding that perfect shade of lipgloss?"

Branwen got up and snatched the bag from Dex. She shoved it back into her pack, then started gathering up the rest of her stuff.

"Branwen—" Daphna said. She didn't know what she wanted to say, but it didn't matter.

"You want to know what's wrong with me?" Branwen snapped. "I'll tell you what's wrong with me. I'm stupid. Okay? I'm *stupid*. I can barely do elementary school math. When I read something—anything—I don't remember it."

"Branwen—" Daphna tried again.

"Well, guess what! I didn't make myself this way. *God* made me stupid! I can't succeed in life with what he put into my head. Am I supposed to just accept that? He also made me the most beautiful girl people I meet have ever seen! Am I supposed to say thanks, but I'll pass when the world wants to give me whatever I want because of that? I DON'T THINK SO!"

"Branwen—"

"People work with what they have, you snotty little twit! You do it too! You sold out your brain to make friends, and that's no different—"

"Oh, my God."

Branwen was stuffing the last item into her bag, but Daphna saw what it was before it went in. The famous little black dress she wore when she most wanted to impress people. "You knew the arch was there," Daphna realized. "You were only on the ledge because you couldn't get through it. You came down here to—You can't possibly think—"

Branwen had everything packed up now. She found her flashlight, then shined it at Daphna and said, "Words aren't the only things that can work magic." Then she turned and began walking down the branch of the hall that led to the left.

"Branwen!" Daphna realized the gun was still in her hand. She tossed it away.

Dex shone his light after Branwen, but the hall turned quickly. She was already gone. "Did I miss something?" he asked.

"Dex," Daphna said, "Branwen didn't come to trade the Grail. She didn't *have* the Grail. She thinks she's going to survive all this—"

"How?"

"By charming the Devil."

Dexter had nothing to say to this.

"Dex," Daphna asked, "why did you make us take her into the clinic? Tell me the truth."

"Because the Secret Keeper was watching."

"What? Why would—?"

"I wanted to show him I wasn't the Antichrist."

"Oh." Daphna nodded, sadly. She didn't know why tears were suddenly trying to find their way out of her eyes at this of all things. "You're not the Antichrist," she said, fighting them back.

Dexter only shrugged. He hadn't realized this was the truth until he said it.

"And neither am I, for that matter. Let's just forget about Branwen. She's totally mental." Daphna looked at her watch. "We have less than two and a half hours," she said, freshly alarmed. "And we have no idea where we're going."

"Down. We need to go down. Where else?"

"But how?"

"Look." The moment Dex had said 'down,' he'd looked down, and he'd seen that something had been exposed under the dirt where Branwen's supplies had been dropped and reclaimed, a sliver of something that looked like leather.

Squatting, the twins brushed the dirt away from it. They both knew what it was well before they cleared enough to see for sure, but they were not prepared for how big it was. It was nearly six feet long and two or three feet wide.

It was the cover of a book.

CHAPTER FORTY-ONE
Abandon All Hope

"There's something written on it," Daphna said. She and Dex continued swiping dirt away until the words were revealed in giant letters etched into the cover.

"What does it say?"

Daphna stepped back so she could take a broader view. Dex gave her the flashlight, so she swept the light around the words. When she finally processed them, she went pale.

"What?"

"It says, 'Abandon all Hope, ye who enter here.'"

"Fine," Dex said, brushing dirt off his hands. He got up, then leaned back down to pry up the cover's edge.

"Dex," Daphna warned, "that line—It's what's supposedly written on the gates of Hell."

Dex looked up at his sister and shrugged. "Where did you think we were going? *China?*"

"No, but—"

The cover lifted easily, though it was unwieldy because of its size. When Dex had it vertical, he shoved it over. It hit the ground, sending up a cloud of dirt and clay.

The twins looked into the book.

Inside was a set of cobblestone stairs descending into darkness.

"We have no plan," Daphna said, staring into the hole, this new, ominous hole inside the hole they were already too deep inside. Despite how far they'd come, it seemed crazy to walk down those steps. "We have no ideas," she added, a bit louder now. Her pulse was starting to race. Then she shouted, "*We have nothing to work with!* Dad told us there was no such thing as the Devil, Dex! He—!"

"Didn't know about Lilit, either. He didn't know about things that came before him."

"But Dex," Daphna protested, "this—down there. Was it always here? Just empty all this time? He—*It* wasn't, right? It was in that Book, locked in that Book in Heaven. I think he brought all this down with him. Which means all the stories everyone tells about the Devil—"

"Stories," Dex snapped, feeling his pulse spike now, too. "I'm sick of stories!" He looked down at the golden book in his hand, at the golden key in its cover, then back at his sister, who'd gone quiet at the look in his eyes.

"No, Dex."

"I'm tired of this, Daphna. I am sick and tired off all this guessing. Let's just open the book and see what the hell it actually is!"

Daphna put her hand out, but she did not try to reach for Dexter or the book. "No," she warned. "Dex—it's not worth it. You know what Mr. G said. Just *reading* the Name could kill us. And who knows what that might do to our ribs."

"But you said yourself that story was only meant to keep people from—"

"But we don't know that!"

"We don't know anything! We. Never. Know. Anything!"

"Dex, breathe," Daphna counseled, both hands up now because he had one of his on the key.

Dexter tried to breathe. But he was so tired. They might very well have the power in their hands right now to put an end to all of this—to set everything right. *Forever.*

"There are two of us," Dex said. "Let me try. Maybe the Name is protected by some sort of spell, like The Book of Nonsense was, so maybe I'll be the one who can read it. If I'm wrong, you go on with the book."

"That's ridiculous!" Daphna insisted. "And Nora is down there somewhere! *With the Devil, Dex!* The Devil! We just need a plan. We need to think a second. What do we know about the Devil? I mean, besides the red skin and the horns and the pitchfork." Dex was listening, so Daphna kept talking, breathless though she was. "He was supposedly an angel," she remembered, thinking fast. "I think God's favorite angel maybe, but he wouldn't bow down to God, or to man I think in some versions. He tempts people, tries to lead them away from God, though some people think he still serves God, that he actually roots for you not to be tempted, but he tempts you anyway because that's his job. I guess, like they said on the news, some say he brought death into the world. I don't know much about that. Maybe Jesus took the book out of Heaven because it could undo death for people. So they could live forever. Maybe that's how the story got mixed up with the ones about the Philosopher's Stone. They say Jesus promises eternal life, right? Maybe it was literal, eternal life, here, on Earth—but maybe his followers didn't think that was wise, so they hid it."

Dexter's hand was still on the key. He was staring at it, but he was still listening.

"But maybe it's the opposite of the Philosopher's Stone," Daphna rambled. "Maybe the Devil can kill everyone in the world with it—if he hates man. Oh! He's supposed to have started a rebellion against God in Heaven and was 'cast down' or something like that—locked up, I guess—for his pride. Yeah, that's his big thing, his 'overweening pride.' Dex! See! We aren't abandoning everything!"

Dex looked up and said, "What do you mean?"

"His pride! His terrible *pride*. Do you know that saying, 'Pride comes before the fall?' That's something to work with!" It wasn't much, but Daphna could see Dex considering it all. "Try to let your breath touch your core for just a second," she urged, "then—"

"How much time do we have?" Dex asked. He took his hand off the key.

Daphna looked at her watch. "Two hours and ten minutes," she said. Her heart was still pounding.

"Do you hear that?"

Daphna cocked her ear toward the hole. "Yes," she said. "That scratching. It's coming from down there."

Dex nodded. He clutched the Grail a bit tighter and stepped onto the first stone step framed by the massive book in the ground. The steps were cracked and uneven, but didn't look too difficult to manage. He took the next step, and the one after that.

Daphna shined the light over her brother's shoulder so he could see. It focused for a moment on the glowing book in his hand. She shuddered with equal parts terror and relief, then followed him down.

The steps seemed to go on forever down a narrow, sharply angled incline. Daphna moved ahead of Dex so she could use the flashlight more effectively. Every few minutes she checked her watch and then urged them to hurry on. The noxious smoke billowed up around them, and that scratching sound got louder and louder, it seemed, with every step.

They didn't bother mentioning it. They both just tried to breathe and step.

Breathe and step.

Breathe and step.

Breathe and step.

CHAPTER FORTY-TWO
No Corner

Almost exactly an hour later, the twins reached the bottom, which was simply another corridor with hollowed out shelves holding more horrid books. Without comment, they walked through it, trying to avoid even glancing at the vile things. Soon, Daphna saw that the hall branched to both the left and right. She indicated left, glancing back at Dex, who nodded. She made the turn.

But the moment she made it, Daphna knew something was wrong. She stopped and looked back to make sure Dex came around the corner, too.

But there was no corner anymore.

"Dex!" Daphna cried. She ran back down the hall and found it branched off in half a dozen directions. Frantic, she took one randomly and ran down it screaming her brother's name. When she didn't find him, she took another random hall, then another, until she was simply running blindly, making turns, wailing.

She stopped.

Books still surrounded her, but they sat on shelves, real wooden shelves. Daphna looked down and saw her feet stood upon a wooden floor.

Daphna walked ahead, looking left and right, blinking. Her mind was playing tricks on her. She couldn't be in the ABC, the bookstore where this all began.

She took a turn and stopped again.

There in front of her was a curtain blocking the entrance to a cubby made of books.

It couldn't be.

"Come in! Come in," croaked a ragged, rasping voice. "I'd love to have a word with you."

The fumes had gone to her head—she was hallucinating. *Can you be hallucinating if you know you are hallucinating?*

Daphna pushed aside the curtain to find Asterius

Rash, the scheming old blind man. He was wearing his brown robe and sitting at his desk, exactly the way he'd been when she'd peeked into the cubby the day before her thirteenth birthday and saw her hypnotized father hand him the Book of Nonsense.

Rash stroked his long white beard and laughed.

"Where am I?" Daphna demanded. "I can't be here! The store burned! *You* burned!"

"As we once discussed," Rash said, "given infinite time, all things will come to pass. Everything is always and only simply a question of time."

"No!" Daphna screamed. "No! You are not real!"

Rash laughed again, that same crackling chortle. "Nevertheless," he said. "Nevertheless."

"No!" Daphna screamed again. This time, she spun round and burst back through the curtain.

She was on a playground. Pops were skipping rope.

Daphna found herself sitting on a balance beam with a book, pretending to read but actually looking longingly on.

A pretty Pop girl in a perfect outfit approached holding a spiral notebook. Daphna didn't know her name.

"Daph," she whispered. *"Can you help me with my homework? I mean, I know the stuff—I just didn't have time to write it up."* When Daphna took the notebook, she said, *"You rule for doing to this. You're such a good reader! Love your hair today, by the way."*

Another girl was suddenly there, another Pop, with another notebook. *"Me too,"* she whispered. *"Love your shoes, by the way."*

Then there were more girls, more and more girls with more and more notebooks. *"We do, too!"* they whispered. *"Love your top."*

"Love your jeans."

"Love your look!"

Frantic, Daphna stood up and pushed her way through the growing crowd, heading for the school's front door. She burst through it.

She was on a private stage, standing in front of a microphone.

Daphna looked back and saw the curtain running along the back wall. Then she looked out at the audience of Pops watching her with wide eyes.

Teal's house. Her private theater.

Daphna looked up and saw the bucket of cleanser, but she couldn't move when the rope attached to it, the rope running behind the curtain, was pulled.

The bucket tipped.

But cleanser didn't fall on Daphna's head.

Books did.

First, it was just a few, but more followed, and then suddenly thousands of books were falling, and Daphna couldn't move to avoid them.

The Pops laughed. There were hundreds of them out there. No, thousands—*hundreds* of thousands—all shrieking with laughter.

"This didn't happen!" Daphna screamed when the books piled up to her neck. "I hate you all! I have always hated you all!" Out of her mind, she fought her way free from the pile and ran at the curtain where Branwen was hiding. She was going to strangle her with the rope she'd pulled.

But when Daphna tore the curtain aside, she found herself once again in front of Asterius Rash, back in his claustrophobic little cubby.

"You are the stronger one," Rash said, looking at Daphna with his ugly, blind eyes.

There was something in the old man's tone that gave Daphna pause. "What—what do you mean?" she asked, struggling to catch her breath.

"Your courage is to be commended, Ms. Wax, but there comes a time when one must recognize the difference between fearlessness and foolishness. Now is the moment to reconsider your foolish errand before it is too late. Your boyfriend is alive, and that is your primary concern. Your mothers are dead—there is no changing that. The scientist—I'm sorry, but there must be sacrifices. Your brother will not be able to face this. As I said, you are stronger one."

"But—"

"At all costs, the Grail cannot be put into the Dragon's hands. Take it and find your way out of the Pit before he finds *you*."

"But the Grail—" Daphna protested, "we have to find a way to destroy it, and only the fire—The Dragon's breath—"

"Nonsense!" Rash growled. "Stories! Lies are

spread, even beyond the veil! Lies that led you here like a horse to water!"

"But—"

"Having crossed over does not render one immune to deceit!" Rash raged. "Where there is language, young lady, there are lies! You were fools to bring the Grail here! Dupes and fools! I assure you that what I tell you is what your mothers want, all three of them."

Daphna went weak in the knees at the thought of abandoning Dr. Fludd, even if she were willing to sacrifice her life.

"Take the Grail out of this hellhole. Take it back to the Templars and let them hide it somewhere new. It is what they do. He will never venture out while it exists beyond his reach."

"But—" Daphna said, "the Name."

"The Name?" Rash roared. "The *Name?* The Grail contains no Name! You know nothing, ignorant girl! The Book of all Books houses the Divine Sparks!"

audience of Pops watching her with wide eyes.

Teal's house. Her private theater.

Daphna looked up and saw the bucket of cleanser, but she couldn't move when the rope attached to it, the rope running behind the curtain, was pulled.

The bucket tipped.

But cleanser didn't fall on Daphna's head.

Books did.

First, it was just a few, but more followed, and then suddenly thousands of books were falling, and Daphna couldn't move to avoid them.

The Pops laughed. There were hundreds of them out there. No, thousands—*hundreds* of thousands—all shrieking with laughter.

"This didn't happen!" Daphna screamed when the books piled up to her neck. "I hate you all! I have always hated you all!" Out of her mind, she fought her way free from the pile and ran at the curtain where Branwen was hiding. She was going to strangle her with the rope she'd pulled.

But when Daphna tore the curtain aside, she found herself once again in front of Asterius Rash, back in his claustrophobic little cubby.

"You are the stronger one," Rash said, looking at Daphna with his ugly, blind eyes.

There was something in the old man's tone that gave Daphna pause. "What—what do you mean?" she asked, struggling to catch her breath.

"Your courage is to be commended, Ms. Wax, but there comes a time when one must recognize the difference between fearlessness and foolishness. Now is the moment to reconsider your foolish errand before it is too late. Your boyfriend is alive, and that is your primary concern. Your mothers are dead—there is no changing that. The scientist—I'm sorry, but there must be sacrifices. Your brother will not be able to face this. As I said, you are stronger one."

"But—"

"At all costs, the Grail cannot be put into the Dragon's hands. Take it and find your way out of the Pit before he finds *you*."

"But the Grail—" Daphna protested, "we have to find a way to destroy it, and only the fire—The Dragon's breath—"

"Nonsense!" Rash growled. "Stories! Lies are

spread, even beyond the veil! Lies that led you here like a horse to water!"

"But—"

"Having crossed over does not render one immune to deceit!" Rash raged. "Where there is language, young lady, there are lies! You were fools to bring the Grail here! Dupes and fools! I assure you that what I tell you is what your mothers want, all three of them."

Daphna went weak in the knees at the thought of abandoning Dr. Fludd, even if she were willing to sacrifice her life.

"Take the Grail out of this hellhole. Take it back to the Templars and let them hide it somewhere new. It is what they do. He will never venture out while it exists beyond his reach."

"But—" Daphna said, "the Name."

"The Name?" Rash roared. "The *Name?* The Grail contains no Name! You know nothing, ignorant girl! The Book of all Books houses the Divine Sparks!"

CHAPTER FORTY-THREE
Doors of Perception

When Dexter reached the corner Daphna had turned—or thought he had—it simply wasn't there. Somehow, he was at a dead end. He put his hands on the dirt wall and turned around, confused. He shook his head, trying to stay calm, imagining he was only momentarily disoriented. He must have zoned out for a minute while walking—something he used to do all the time. It was only his horrid sense-of-direction. He just needed a moment to reorient himself.

Dex closed his eyes to clear his mind, then turned around.

When he opened them again, he found himself standing in a carpeted hallway, lined on both sides with doors, real doors.

This was not possible. How could he be at the Rest and Rehabilitation Home?

Dex turned to look at the door just next to his shoulder.

It was number 306.

Dex decided not to freak out, or melt down, or even be surprised. So he was suddenly back in the R & R. *Why not?* He opened the door and saw his supposedly one-and-only true friend, his wise, white-haired old tutor—the treacherous backstabbing liar and user of users, Ruby Scharlach. She was sitting on her couch, sipping tea. The intricate map of lines on her face creased when she smiled at Dex.

"This is Hell," Dex said, stepping inside, holding the Grail to his chest. "So it makes sense that you're here."

"Perhaps," Ruby conceded. "But it's yours."

"I hope you rot here forever!" Dex spat. "And if you think you're getting your hands on this—" he held up the golden book—"it'll be over my dead body. And even then you won't get it. It'll be over my dead soul!"

With this, Dex spun round, ripped open the door, which had somehow closed behind him, and stepped into the hall.

Dexter ran down the long corridor. Doors on both sides flew past in a blur, but it wasn't long before he knew it would never end. He turned and looked behind him. It now stretched out of sight that way as well.

Dex turned, ripped open the door he was standing next to, and rushed through it.

He was standing in a playground. A ring of kids, little kids—fourth graders?—stood around him.

"He's got a book, and he can't read!" one of the kids jeered.

"What are you gonna do with it," another laughed, "eat it?"

"Spell cat!" someone yelled.

"No," Dex said. He was breathing hard, trying not to cry. This was before he learned to go stony in the face of teasing.

"C'mon! It's *'cat'!"* another kid pressed. "I bet he couldn't spell it if we gave him two letters."

"If we gave him *three!"*

"Cat! Cat! Cat!" the kids chanted. *"Meeeeeow!"*

Dex turned away from the ring of taunters and bumped into something. He turned, hoping it was the door, but it was a tree. And when he turned around again, someone grabbed him around the neck, lifted him off the ground, and slammed him into it.

He was in Gabriel Park.

Emmet—giant, red-eyed, burned up Emmet—had him by the throat. The ring of kids stood a safe distance behind Asterius Rash's bodyguard, pointing and laughing and calling, "Cat! Cat! Meeeeeow!"

Emmet slammed Dex into the tree again, making his eyes roll back, then dropped him.

Dex found himself on the floor in the hall in front of room 306, still holding the Grail.

He got up and went inside.

Ruby set her teacup down on the coffee table and dabbed her lips with a napkin. "Dexy," she said. "I don't want that silly thing. What would I need with an empty book?

An empty book! Dex laughed at the ridiculous lie. Compared to the Book of Letters, the Book of

Nonsense was as powerful as a collection of nursery rhymes—and the Aleph? A toy. And now he was supposed to believe the Holy Grail was a book of blank pages. He turned, opened the door again, then strode out of the room.

Back in the hall, all he saw were doors again. He tore open the one directly across the hall this time, but did not rush through it.

He found himself looking into Ruby's apartment. She winked at him over her tea.

Dex ran down the hallway in the other direction, but he could see the numbers on all the doors were the same: 306—every one.

The hall terminated in a dead-end. There was a door there: Room 306.

Shoulders slumping, Dex opened it and went inside.

"Dexy, Dexy, Dexy," Ruby said. "Come in! Have a seat. We must catch up!"

Dex stayed where he was. "This *is* my Hell," he realized. "You're here so you can lie to me for the rest of eternity. So I can think about what a stupid, gullible, needy little pants-pissing chump I was. Am. *Was*—forever."

"That's not what I signed up for," Ruby replied. "I can promise you that."

"Well, you're lying about the Grail," Dex said. "It can't be empty." He looked down at it again. "It took us here from the Well of Souls."

"Oh, honey," Ruby said, not without apparent sympathy. "You're here because the *Red Dragon* brought you here. That book had nothing to do with it."

"But it—"

"It shines because *he* wants it to shine."

Dex stared at the book harder now, trying to see right through the glowing gold cover.

"Though I suppose 'empty' is not quite accurate," Ruby conceded. "The Grail itself is a symbol, certainly, which is anything but empty. It's a very, very powerful symbol—the most powerful symbol in the world."

"I don't believe you."

"Open it. You'll find nothing."

Dex looked at the key. But he didn't turn it. He

didn't dare. Ruby was a liar—the biggest liar in the world.

"I won't insult you by offering to open it myself," Ruby said. "But listen to me, Dexter. I don't want to be here. I take no pleasure in causing you pain. I am past all that. I am past all desires but one: I want to rest."

Dex was put off balance by the sadness in the old woman's voice. He'd never heard it before in all the times they'd talked. "How could it be empty?" he whined.

"That book, the Holy Grail, is the single greatest incarnation of hope ever known," Ruby explained. "It was Jesus' most brilliant contribution to the world. He instructed Joseph of Arimathea to create a symbol that would provide enduring hope for mankind, *all* of mankind, hope that there was something out there that could save them one day. Its power lies precisely in the fact that it is hidden, and will always be hidden. You must take it out of here. Find the Templars and let them hide it again. Real hope, Dexter, must always hide."

"But if it's just an empty book," Dex said, "there'd be no harm in giving it to the Dragon."

"Except that he will take it out of the pit and destroy it in front of the entire world. He will destroy hope forever, which will make establishing his dominion over man effortless. There will be no resistance."

"But—but—" Dex stuttered. Possibilities were tumbling through his mind. "We have a plan. We're going to give it to him, so we can get The Book of the Living back, but then we're going to destroy the Grail. So, he won't be able to do that, destroy hope, I mean. We could convince people that the book was never really found."

"And this plan? How will you carry it out?"

"We're not exactly sure yet."

"And yet you risk the entire world?"

Dex was unable to meet his old tutor's deeply critical eyes. He knew he was risking the world for Nora.

"Yes," he said. Then he turned, opened the door, and stepped back through it one last time.

CHAPTER FORTY-FOUR
Out of the Blue

"The Divine Sparks?" Daphna said. She couldn't handle another possibility. Her head was going to explode, but—that phrase rang a bell.

"Let me tell you the truth," Rash offered, calming down. "One benefit of my position is knowing the actual truth."

"Why should I believe anything you say?"

"Because, child," Rash said, almost softly. "I have discovered myself to be but a bit player on stage far too grand for me. I want—to rest. If you are of no use to him, he will have no more use for me."

Daphna, eyes wide and wary, nodded.

"Before creation," Rash began, "God was everywhere, manifesting in an all-encompassing Light. To initiate life, He contracted Himself to a single point of infinite density and energy, then exploded outward, creating space for our universe."

"The Big Bang," Daphna said.

"In the empty space, God created vessels, but they shattered when the Divine Light flowed into them. The fragments descended into the world of matter—our world: shards imbued with the Divine Sparks."

"Right," Daphna said, finally remembering where she'd learned this: on the back of a book in Mr. G's house. "It's people's job to find and free the lost Light, to let the Sparks rise back up to God—to repair the world."

"Indeed," Rash confirmed. "But the job was done."

"Jesus did it," Daphna guessed.

"His gift," Rash said, "was to see the Divine where it dwelled. He collected the shards. He gathered the Light—into himself. He made himself a Holy Vessel, which gave him some mystical powers."

"But—"

"He was a man. When he was killed, the Light flowed out of him. But it was captured in another vessel by—"

"Joseph—in the *Book!*" Daphna could see it now. "That's why it glows! It's not really a book at all. That's why it came to be thought of as a grail!"

"It's a vessel of Divine Light," Rash confirmed. "And if the Dragon obtains it, he will snuff that Light out forever. The world will be plunged into darkness—darknesses of many terrible kinds."

"But why didn't—?"

"Jesus set free the Light? Because it would be blinding to mankind. Jesus instructed Joseph to hide the Grail until the world was ready to see the Light. The Dragon fears the Light because one day man might be ready for it. As long as the vessel is in the world, the Dragon will remain below, hiding in the dark."

"But—"

"Find your brother," Rash instructed. "Take the book out of this pit. Find the Templars and let them protect the Sparks until the world is ready to see the Light."

Daphna looked into the old man's dead eyes for a long moment, wondering what they saw. She didn't know what to say. She didn't know what to do. But whatever it was she was going to decide, she didn't need Asterious Rash's approval for it. She turned around and walked through the curtain one last time.

Once again, Daphna found herself in the foul-smelling tunnels with their hollowed out shelves full of sinister books. She was so relieved to be away from Rash, that it was almost comforting to hear that scritching and scratching sound again. She looked behind her and saw that the curtain was gone. Then she looked at her watch, panicked, and screamed for her brother. She only screamed his name once, though. After that, she nearly choked at the sight of the figure who suddenly appeared from around a corner a few dozen yards down the hall.

Dead Face.

It was the assassin who'd opened that locked book in Heaven and set the Dragon free. He'd been vaporized in the Light, but here he was.

Of course, here he was.

"Dex!" Daphna screamed again as she took off running the other way. Dead Face, his pale, expressionless expression as cold as ever, walked slowly after her.

"Dex! *Dex!*"

As Daphna sprinted by the shelves, books whipped open on both sides of her. Pages burst from their spines, forcing Daphna to run through a sharp and stinging blizzard. She managed to reach a corner where the books remained closed, but once around it she stopped in her tracks again.

Brother Joe was there, the monk who'd sought demons. He grinned and began walking toward her. "I found him!" he cried. "I found my true master at last!"

Daphna turned and ran down still another hall.

She stopped yet again, this time at the sight of still another familiar face, but this one a joy to see: Mrs. Tapi. The old woman smiled and pointed down a hall. Daphna ran that way. She could hear Dead Face and Brother Joe giving chase, but in the new hall she found Mr. Bergelmir—The Dwarves were there! Her old folks' reading group! The ancient Council that fought against Asterius Rash! They were here, and they were helping!

Daphna raced down the hall Mr. B pointed to, and there she was directed to another by Mr. Tumbainot. Mrs. Deucalion sent her down a hall after that, and Mr. Dwyfan was there to point her to yet one more. Mr. Hina directed her to a final turn.

After Daphna made that turn, she could not hear anyone at all.

She stopped and hunched over to catch her breath.

And that's when she saw the snake.

Dex called his sister's name, and when he got no response, he took off running through the maze.

He only had to take a single turn to find her.

Daphna was standing there like a statue. A massive snake was rearing up over her, ready to strike.

Dex knew without a doubt it was the demon they'd destroyed.

It was Lilit.

"Daphna!" Dex cried. His voice seemed to snap

her out of the trance she was in.

Slowly, she began backing away from the snake. When she reached Dex, together, they turned and ran, but the hall they chose was a dead end.

They were trapped, and the snake was there, slithering toward them, hissing.

The twins sank to the ground and cowered together.

And now it was right there, looming over them, poised with its mouth wide open, its fangs dripping venom.

Dex gripped the Grail. He put his hand on the key.

"No!" Daphna insisted. Just then something slid into her knees.

Another book.

Another book with a key.

The snake reared back, spitting and hissing.

Daphna turned the key and opened this new book.

Lilit, the snake, moved to strike. But instead, it suddenly jerked upright and produced a hideous scream. The twins could see why. Its body was becoming insubstantial, like a ghost's—and it was being sucked into the book.

Lilit screeched and hissed while she was taken, but it was useless. When the monster was fully contained, Daphna slammed the cover and turned the key to lock it inside.

Trembling, the twins gaped at the book, their gift from out of the blue.

But then Dexter looked up and saw who had bestowed it upon them. "Daphna," he said, his face gone white.

Daphna looked up and saw him, too.

It was Milton Wax.

It was *Adam*, the world's first man.

It was their father.

CHAPTER FORTY-FIVE
A Prison

The twins got to their feet and stared at their dad, neither able to react to his having saved them—or even to his being there at all. He regarded them with weary eyes under drooping bushy brows. He seemed a bit hunched.

It was their father as they knew him, creaky old Milton Wax.

But they were wary.

"I was wrong," he told them. "I know that now. I know that one can love God too much—or that to love Him too much is in fact not to love him enough."

This nearly melted Daphna. "Are—are you—?"

"I did not survive the fall at Eden's edge," Milton said. "And I am so sorry I tried to take you with me. The Dragon—he brought us all here, all of us who've done damage. He took us before he began to burn the Books of Blessed Rest. But he does not bother with us until he needs us. He is only concerned with the living."

"Nora!" Dex screamed, scanning the halls in all directions. "Nora!"

"She will not come," Milton sighed. She is with him, below, in his personal library.

Daphna looked at her watch. Less than an hour—if they still planned to take the Grail to the Devil.

"Then let's go already!" Dex insisted.

"Yes!" Milton agreed. "I will help you defeat the Beast! *This* is how I will show my love for God."

"You *knew* God!" Daphna cried, suddenly seizing on a possible solution. "You *spoke* with Him! Do you know His Name? Can you pronounce it? Can you bring him here that way? We don't have much time! An hour! They're going to drop a bomb—!"

"Do you really believe that God can be summoned like a dog?" Milton asked, his face gone dark. "I made this mistake once," he added. "I will not make it again."

"It doesn't matter," Dex said, turning to his sister. "There's nothing in the Grail, anyway. It's empty."

"What?"

"Ruby told me—just before—" Dex said, waving down the hall of books. "She says we have to take the book out and hide it because even though it's empty, it's the most important symbol of hope in the world. She hates this place, too, and wants to help."

"Ruby?" Daphna said, amazed. "You—? I saw Rash!" She turned to her father. "He said the Grail houses the Divine Sparks—that Jesus collected them. He—he said we have to take it out of here, too, because the Dragon will snuff them out forever—and all hope for a better world with them."

"Rash?" Dex asked. "You saw—Divine what?"

"There are too many stories!" Daphna raged. She was losing her mind, and no kind of breathing was going to help. "We've been told that book possesses power because the pages caught Jesus' blood! We've been told it has the Secret Name of God. That it doesn't have the Secret Name of God! That it's the Book of Divine Sparks! That it's the Book of Blood and the Book of Death! We've been told the world will never be safe unless it's destroyed and that only the Dragon's breath can destroy it. And now everyone's telling us to take it back out of this infernal pit and hide it? But if we do that, bombs are going to fall! Nuclear bombs! HOW ARE WE SUPPOSED TO KNOW WHAT TO DO!"

"No," Milton said, surprising the twins. "You must not take the Grail out of this pit."

"But—!"

"Before God removed Himself, before he withdrew from the world, he surely would have known what would take place. He would have foreseen this disaster, and he would have planned for it. He told me—He told me all would be well with the world. He promised."

"Well, it hasn't been!" the twins both shouted. On this point, there was not the slightest bit of disagreement between them.

"It's a trap."

"What?" Daphna asked, but then she understood. "It's a prison," she said, turning to Dex. "The

Grail is a prison, like the one we just used. Like the one the Dragon was in. All the books with keys are. If he opens it, he'll get sucked in—like Lilit just did."

"Yes and no," said Milton. "There would be little use in putting him back into that which did not hold him."

"What do you mean?" Daphna asked.

"Jesus took what you call the Holy Grail from Heaven," Milton explained. "It is one of many locking books meant for malevolent souls. He took an *empty* one."

"It *is* empty?" Dex cried.

"No, it is not."

The twins looked at each other.

"Jesus took the book because it had to be here, on Earth, so that one day The Dragon would seek it, so that one day you two would bring it to him. After forty days of preparing his followers for what to do with the Holy Grail, Jesus opened it himself."

The twins' mouths dropped open.

"The book has been hidden ever since in anticipation of this moment, the moment the Dragon, imagining himself the master of God, will meet his match."

"But that means—" Dex started to say, looking down at the golden book in his hand.

"That the Secret Keeper was right," Daphna said, finishing the thought. "We *are* the Antichrists. When we hand the book to the Devil and he opens it—Jesus will return."

"And when the bombs fall anyway," Dex added, "we'll have ushered in the Apocalypse."

"You must hurry," Milton urged. "Give the Grail to the Dragon. The key was made in Heaven to turn only by his hand."

"You mean we couldn't have opened if we tried?" Dex asked.

"That is correct," Milton confirmed. "Now hurry. You must waste no more time, especially if you wish to save your loved ones."

"But we don't know where his library is," Dex complained. "We know it's at the bottom, but we have no idea how to get there. We have no idea where we are. These shelves go on forever! And we're running out of time! We have thirty minutes! AND WHAT'S

THAT SCRATCHING!"

"You have made your way down," Milton said. "Follow the sound, and you will find him. I must go. If I am discovered advising you, things will go badly for us all." Then he smiled at the twins, and they both saw the heart of the father they used to know and love.

Milton Adam Wax nodded, then vanished before their eyes.

The twins looked at each other once again, wordlessly deciding not to discuss the fact that they'd just seen their dead father, that they'd been saved by the man who'd tried to kill them before his death. Instead, they began making their way through the halls of books, choosing the ones in which the scratching sound seemed loudest.

They kept to the center of the corridors, carefully eying every book they passed. But the books let them be. They walked in silence, both thinking about the risk they now both seemed prepared to take.

The scratching was very loud now.

They turned a corner and stopped. There was another archway, this one leading, it seemed, outside. Slightly fresher air was flowing in from beyond it.

The twins passed under the arch and found themselves in the open bottom of the pit. It was hard at first to make out anything with the smoke swirling around. There was a moment of shared panic when a looming shadow made them fear the Dragon was upon them, but a gust of circling wind revealed it to be the twisted remains of the downed helicopter. They approached it carefully. The metal carcass was still smoldering.

The twins looked up. A glimmer of sky showed through the smoke thousands of feet above. Wind swept the smoke a way for a moment, revealing tiny black shapes against the sky.

"Planes," Dex said.

"Dex!"

Daphna was hurrying through the smoke to a figure crumpled on the ground just beyond the helicopter's crushed fuselage.

"It's Picker!" she called. "He's dead." She didn't know why it upset her so much, but it did.

"He's got your book," Dex observed when he reached the body. The library book was somehow still in the little man's hand. When Daphna hesitated, he said, "Don't you want it?"

"Ah, yes," Daphna said. "Okay, yes. It's just—" She leaned over Picker apprehensively, then snatched the book out of his hand—or tried to. It was hard to pull free at first, which made her want to wretch. She yanked harder, and it came free.

"Look," Dex said. He was pointing into the smoke where it seemed to be clearing a bit.

Daphna looked.

There, across from the arch they'd come through, stood two guards in red robes holding spears.

They were guarding a flaming gate.

CHAPTER FORTY-SIX
The Plan

The guards saw the twins and immediately opened the gate. The flames swarming on its bars seemed to have no effect on them.

"Okay," Daphna said after a deep breath. But then an awful thought struck her. "What if he takes the book, but doesn't open it?" she asked. "We still don't have a plan!"

"Yes, we do," Dex said, surprising her. "We're going in there, and we're going to give him the Grail. And if he doesn't open it, we're going to make him. We're going to get him really mad by tweaking his pride somehow—mad enough to open it, anyway. And when Jesus comes out and it all hits the fan, we're going to find Nora, and Dr. Fludd, and Quinn's parents, and even Wren—and maybe even Nora's crazy father—and then we are going to get out of this hellhole as quickly as possible and send the planes away. *That's* the plan."

Daphna looked at Dex, into his fierce eyes. That was not much of a plan, but it would have to do. "Okay," she said. "Okay. Let's do it."

Dex nodded, and so the twins approached the gate. They stopped for a moment when they neared the flames leaping off the bars, but it quickly became clear that they gave off no heat. The guards stood in silence.

The twins walked between them, right into the fire, and they didn't stop when it enveloped them. And they kept walking, right on through the flames, following the scratching sounds, which were very, very loud now.

They were close.

The flames began to flag, and then they were gone, and when the twins' eyes adjusted, they found themselves in cozy, wood-paneled library, facing a man in corduroy pants and a tweed jacket with patches on the sleeves. He had small, round, wire-rimmed glasses and salt and pepper sideburns. He was sitting at a desk, scratching away on old parchment paper with a large quill pen.

"Ah!" the man said, looking up with a warm smile. "Welcome to my little writer's garret!" His face was open and inviting, his eyes lively and intense. He set the quill pen down next to an inkwell, then put the paper he was writing on in a basket filled with other sheets. Then he turned his focus to Dex and said, "And you've brought my book!" His voice was anything but threatening. It was the voice of a scholar. He held out his hand. "May I have it? Why don't you just set it on the desk here."

"You're—" Daphna fumbled, "you're the Dragon? The—the Devil?"

"Poppycock!" the man scoffed. "Children's stories! There is no Devil! Listen," he said, leaning toward Daphna like a professor eager to impart a lesson, "I'm sure you've heard the expression that it's the winners who get to write the history books. We are all storytellers. You, me, and God Almighty, too. It's just that only some of us get to have our stories heard. Am I right, Dexter?"

"Storyteller?" Daphna sneered, watching her brother try to ignore this. She forced a less-than-convincingly cruel laugh. "You're just a hack who couldn't write his way onto a discount rack."

The Devil smiled, revealing perfect teeth. "Have you wondered why all the books?" he asked, evidently not bothered a bit by Daphna's first attack on his pride. "Why do you think the Big Guy is so big on books? Surely, you've wondered! I know you have, Dexter."

Neither twin responded to this, but they both wanted to hear the answer.

"Because you are His stories," the Devil told them. "He created this world with words, and it is through words that you comprehend what little you do of it. You are nothing but words. There is no life without words, and books are their temple. To be a Storyteller is to be a god. I am a god."

"You're a loser," Daphna said, eyeing her brother so he would help her. "You got locked up for being a loser. You've missed the last few thousand years!

Now you're hiding down here because you're afraid of what's up there."

"Take it," Dex said, holding out the Holy Grail. "I'll bet you can't even read what's in it."

Again, the smile. The Devil pushed back his chair and stood up. "I'll be happy to read it to you, Dex," he said. "It's got quite a story. Set it on the desk, please and thank you."

Holding the book out, Dexter took a hesitant step forward, but before he could set it down, Daphna snatched it out of his hand.

The Devil sat back down. He seemed pleased by the drama unfolding before him.

"What are you doing?" Dex cried when he'd recovered from the shock. "He said he would read what's in it!"

Daphna took a step back. She tossed her library book to the floor, then whisked the Grail behind her back to protect it with both hands. It was that smile. Something had been bugging her since the moment her father vanished. And now she knew what it was— the way he'd made her trust him. "I'm sorry, Dex," she said, talking fast again, "but it's all too perfect. Don't you see? Everyone we *distrust* told us to take it away. Everyone we *trust* told us to take it to him. It's how a really clever writer would fool us!"

"Fiddlesticks!" said the Devil, sounding highly amused. He leaned back and put a foot up on the desk.

"*Nora* told me to give it to him," Dexter shouted. "But—!"

"I don't care about what anyone else said, Daphna! I didn't care when they said it, either!"

"I know Nora is important to you, Dex, but we can't risk the entire world for her. The truth is you hardly know her."

"But you were prepared to risk the world because a boy you hardly know *might* still be alive? *Wait a minute,*" Dex said, his eyes narrowing to slits. "Quinn's awake, isn't he? That's why you didn't mind when Picker swiped that library book. That's why you didn't care about finding it again, either! You don't want me to take this risk BECAUSE YOU DON'T HAVE TO!"

"Oh, this is good," the Devil said. "This is very good. By the way," he added, "it's twenty minutes to sundown."

Daphna looked at her watch to find the countdown at exactly twenty minutes. She looked up at her brother, but he didn't seem to care. He was moving toward her. "Try to reach her," Daphna urged, taking another step back. "Just one more time, Dex. He can't take the book from us. If he could, he would have the second we entered the pit! No one down here can touch us because they aren't substantial—not yet, anyway. Not even his fire can hurt us!"

"Perhaps you'd be interested in a trade," the Devil said, standing up. He walked to a bookshelf and pointed to a row of richly bound volumes. "I have some remarkable one-of-a-kinds here. Take this one, for example." He pulled one out and read its title. "The Book of Forgiveness. Now doesn't that sound appropriate right now?" The Devil set it down on his desk, then took another book down. "Here we have the Book of Redemption and Deliverance. Can come in very handy! Oh, the Book of Sustenance and Abundance is a boon." He took that one down, too, and set them both on the desk as well. "Let me know when something strikes your fancy," he invited, turning back once again to the shelf.

"Dex," Daphna plead, "the Grail must be destroyed."

"Perhaps this recent acquisition might be of interest, damaged though it is."

The twins looked. The Devil now held the Book of the Living. The knife Dex had driven into it was still buried in its pages. The back cover and one loose page flopped open when he set it on the desk.

The twins stared at it, momentarily mesmerized.

"Did I mention it's seventeen minutes to sundown?"

Now the twins looked back at each other.

"And of course, these other recent acquisitions might be of interest to you as well," the Devil said. "Real finds." He pointed to a set of books high on a shelf and read their spines. "Let's see—What do we have here? This one is called, *Roberta Fludd.*"

Daphna went pale.

"And this one," the Devil continued, sliding a book out, "is called *Nora Jons.*"

"He can read the Name," Daphna warned her

brother, watching his eyes. "I can feel it in my bones! He's going to say the Name, and then something awful is going to happen. *The End* is going to happen—for all of us! We have to take the Grail and just go. It's our only choice!"

Dexter turned to his sister, shaking.

"She's right about the Name, of course," the Devil confirmed. "How could I not know how to pronounce the name of my own twin brother?"

CHAPTER FORTY-SEVEN
Twins

Now Dex looked back at the Devil. Daphna did too. Neither spoke. Neither could.

"But I can assure, you," he said, sliding Nora's Book back onto the shelf, "I will not utter the Name."

"You're His *twin?*" Daphna croaked.

"His *evil* twin—according to Him, anyway." The Devil looked at Dex and added, "Is there not always a Good twin and a Bad twin? Or at least one twin who always thinks so?"

Dex looked at his sister, who was shaking her head. "No, Dex," she said. "Don't let him do this to us."

Dexter charged.

With her hands still behind her back, Daphna had no defense. Dex slammed her into the shelves behind her, and together they fell to the floor.

Dex punched his sister in the stomach. She gasped and balled up, but got her hands into his hair, which she began to yank. She kicked too.

The twins scratched and clawed and kicked and punched until finally Daphna realized something. "I don't love Quinn!" she screamed.

Dex stopped struggling. He sat up, panting. "What?"

"I mean, I might," Daphna wheezed, sitting up, struggling for air. "Someday." She was crying. "But I don't know. How could I? He loves me, and that's not the same. I decided I loved him when I *lost* him. I hoped he would change my life. I made him my Grail."

Dex looked into his sister's eyes and saw in them the pain of self-knowledge, and so he let the pain enter him as well. He bowed his head and said, "Nora—I—me too."

"A *simply abysmal turning point,*" the Devil sighed. He was leaning back with his foot up on his desk again. "A complete and utter flop!" But then he said, oddly, "Thank you, darling. Just set it down."

The twins looked away from the suffering in each other's identical eyes and saw the Holy Grail resting on the Devil's desk. "Isn't she simply—*divine?*" the Devil said.

"I'm sorry," Dex groaned. "I'm so, so sorry."

Branwen was in her black dress and heels, one of which was broken. Though her face was slightly smudged and her hair only partly salvaged, she looked—there was no denying it—beautiful. She looked at Daphna and flashed a vicious, victorious smile.

The Devil smiled at Branwen and said, "Did I not tell you it would end this way?"

"You told me it would end exactly this way," she replied.

"Character *is* plot, my dear—but never mind. I know you don't read." He turned to the twins and said, "As I was saying, your little epiphanies are dreadful. You've murdered the love stories! Unforgivable!"

The twins, still on the floor, were frozen.

"But there's no lack of irony," the Devil continued. "And I am a *big* fan of irony. Here, let me show you what I mean. Would you mind, dear?"

The Devil pointed to Daphna's library book on the floor. Branwen picked it up.

"Page 666, I believe. Second paragraph. Just kidding. Page 121."

Branwen turned to the page and read, "'One thing to keep in mind at all times to avoid being duped by the dia—diabolical—is that angels, like all those who've gone beyond, cannot produce language human ears can—comprehend. They can only communicate with nonverbal signs. Should you find their frequency, you will have to remember what you saw or heard to interpret later.'"

The Devil looked up. Now Daphna groaned. She'd heard the harmonic language of the angels herself! She'd been face-to-face with her mothers in Heaven, and they'd not spoken a single word to her that she could understand. She'd been blinded by her own desperation.

"If I may pile on," the Devil said, lifting the stack of papers from his basket, "and I do so love to pile on—" He flipped through the pages for a moment, then handed one to Branwen. "Read the first line, will you, dear?"

Branwen smiled again at Daphna, a classic Pop smirk, then read, but this time not in her own voice. The voice that came out of her mouth was Quinn's: *Daphna, you will not be able to speak the Name. You will die if you try. Your soul will shrivel and die, and we will never be together. There is a way. A terrible way. The angels believe that if the book were to be destroyed, he who destroyed it would perish with it.*

"No," Daphna moaned. Tears were pouring. She looked at her watch.

Twelve minutes.

"Hold on," the Devil urged. He handed another sheet to Branwen. She read, now in Nora's voice, *Listen to me, Dex. You have nine days to bring me home, to bring us all home. I want to come home. I had no life until I met you. I wasn't even really alive. I want to live, and to live with you in my life. You've given me a reason to have a life."*

"But—" the twins both pled.

"Wait! One more—" He handed over yet another page, this time with a flourish.

Branwen read in the voice of Milton Wax: "I know that now. I know that one can love God too much— or that to love Him too much is in fact not to love him enough."

"Good stuff, no?" the Devil bragged. "I'm rather proud of that bit."

The twins hung their heads.

"Devastating, I know," he said. "Because they're gone. They're *all* gone. Everyone you love is dead. That boy in a coma, too. Dead as a doornail. Dead, dead, dead. Everyone is dead. For some time now, I have been the author of your story, and I have told it very, very well."

This was too much. The twins just sat there on the floor stupefied, once and for all defeated. They both saw Daphna's watch flash ten minutes, but that provoked no feeling whatsoever in either one of them.

The Devil set the Holy Grail on top of the stack of Sacred Books on his desk, then said, "Let's tie up the loose ends, then, shall we?"

"You're not His brother," Daphna muttered.

"I am," the Devil said. "I really am. Let's get to the part when I explain myself before casting you into the Realm of Dead Souls over with, shall we? Obligatory, right? Am I right?"

The twins did not respond.

"God came first. I will admit this. He is the Grand Storyteller. But he got bored, see? One character is boring. No drama. No tension. So he looked into Himself, and he identified the selfish part, the part that wasn't perfect. The part he *feared*. And he separated that part from himself, giving shape to his Antagonist. He learned that there is no life worth living without one.

"He regretted it immediately for I attempted to slay him the first moment I could. To make a long story short, He imprisoned me in the first of His Locked Books. He put me on a shelf, forever. Imagine my surprise when, after being freed in the most fortuitous fashion, I discovered that He'd put the rest of Himself away, too, apparently as a favor to his beloved little creatures." The Devil paused his story there. He looked down at the twins, both still crumpled on the floor.

A few moments later, he said, "I'm waiting."

The twins said nothing. They knew nothing.

"When I was set free," the Devil continued, evidently offering a hint, "what do I find, but that tables have been turned in the most wonderful possible way. I couldn't have written a better ending myself!"

The twins looked at each other as the truth dawned on them, as the magnitude of what they'd done went to work dissolving whatever was left of themselves.

"God," they said together. "*God* is in the Holy Grail."

CHAPTER FORTY-EIGHT
Down Into Darkness

"Excellent!" the Devil cried, clapping for the twins. "Almost there!"

"You mean," Dex said, "we could have just opened the book—at any time—and brought—?"

"A ha! Bravo! Well done! There we are."

The twins collapsed onto their backs and lay that way staring up at the carved ceiling of the Devil's study, seeing nothing.

"Did I mention," the Devil added, "that should you two *somehow* wind up in the Realm of Dead Souls—just in case you happen to be wondering—your ribs would be passed on. No need to worry on that score."

"Okay," Daphna said, suddenly sitting up. "You win." Dexter looked at her when she said this, and she could tell he knew she was up to something. But as she dragged herself to her feet, she stared at him hard, trying to make it clear that it was his move now because that was all the something she had.

"Inevitable, really," the Devil said. "So I wouldn't be too hard on yourselves."

Dexter heard the unmistakable hint of gloating in the Devil's voice. "Show us," he said, getting up, too. "We're ready." And now he looked severely at Daphna, hoping she could tell it meant that's all *he* had.

"Oh, now *this* is simply tragic," the Devil said, but he was already coming around from behind his desk. He approached a shelf across the garret and opened it—a secret door.

The twins approached it as slowly as they could, each eyeing the other desperately, each willing the other to deliver a miracle before The End was upon them once and for all.

Daphna's watch said five minutes.

Nothing was behind the door. It wasn't just darkness—it was the absence of everything. The twins stared into the void, sensing an awful suction beyond the threshold, a suction with the power to crush them to nothing, to whatever was less than nothing.

A black hole.

They were terrified.

"The end of one story and the beginning of another," the Devil observed.

"What kind of story will it be?" both Dexter and Daphna asked at exactly the same time. They exchanged one more look, a look they figured to be their last, but one that meant they were glad their last words were spoken together.

"*Such* a story!" the Devil crowed, his face lighting up. "I will tell a story of *blood!* A story of pain and horror and oceans of blood! I will take the Holy Grail out of the pit and destroy it in front of the men who worship it. They will send fire down upon me from the sky that will usher in their own doom, and I will watch them tear themselves to pieces in the aftermath. Those that survive will take me as their God, and I will reign supreme in a world where the strong devour the weak, a world where even the very idea of beauty no longer exists!"

"Liar!" a voice shrieked.

A book flew through the air in the twins' direction. It went right through the door into the darkness of the Realm of Dead Souls, where it vanished into silence.

Branwen.

Another book flew that almost took Daphna's head off. It hit the shelves behind her and fell to the floor.

"Stop!" the Devil shouted, his voice rising in anger for the first time.

There the twins stood, on the threshold of the Void with the Devil at their side—and there was Branwen in her little black dress, standing at the desk, raging, her gorgeous face contorted, her hand in the air.

Holding the Holy Grail.

"*No!*" the Devil roared.

"Liar!" Branwen screamed again. And then she hurled the Grail right at the Devil's face.

Her aim was poor.

It sailed well over his head, forcing him to reach right into the Void to catch it.

He caught it.

But he lost his balance.

And the Void began to suck him in.

Suddenly he was the Dragon—seven heads, ten flaming horns, vicious talons and tail. One claw clutched the Book, the other the edge of the doorway. Fire burst from its mouths as it struggled, engulfing the twins.

But the twins ignored the flames

The Red Dragon teetered on the brink, flailing.

Dexter reached out and plucked the Grail from its claw.

Daphna picked up the book at her feet—her library book—and slammed the other claw as hard as she could.

And the Devil fell down into darkness.

CHAPTER FORTY-NINE
The Princess of the World

Dexter carefully closed the shelf-door.

"Did that just happen?" Daphna asked. Her watch said two minutes.

"He lied to me," Branwen snarled, still trembling with rage. "He said I was going to be the Princesses of the World! He said I could have it any way I liked. I can't stand the sight of blood!"

Daphna turned to her brother. "Is this funny?" she asked. "Am I allowed to laugh? I think I'm going to laugh."

She didn't, though. Her watch said one minute.

Dex was already at the desk. He pulled the Book of the Living out from under the books Branwen had knocked onto it.

He turned it over and opened the back cover, exposing the single page the knife and its many blades had not penetrated.

Thirty seconds.

Daphna hurried over and took up the Devil's quill pen. She dipped it into his inkwell.

Fifteen seconds.

She started scratching out names.

Chapter Fifty
thumbs-up to the sky
Four hours later, Dexter reached up under the great ash Tree and felt something soft—something alive, if barely. He gently tugged the wings until they came free from the roots they'd tapped, from the nitrogen they were taking from the soil. Daphna took them from him, then placed them on his back. They didn't Join him, but they clung to his skin—just barely. He hoped it would be enough.

Dex hauled himself out of Hellmouth and looked up into the night sky. He could hear the planes, but couldn't see them. He couldn't see the satellite either, but he was sure it was seeing him.

Dex tilted his head back, spread his wings completely one last time, and held a thumbs-up to the sky.

A few seconds later, the sound of planes faded away.

"Okay," Dex said. He got to his knees and helped Daphna climb out. Together, they helped Branwen.

Then Wren.

Then Quinn's parents.

Then Nora and her father, Pastor Jons.

And then, finally, Dr. Fludd.

The moment they were all out, Dexter's wings fell off his back. Daphna scooped them up and tossed them into the pit.

"Noooo!" someone cried. "Come back! Come back!"

Startled, everyone looked up. The voice seemed to be coming from above.

There, hiding among the branches of the great ash, was the Secret Keeper of the Church, waving his fist at the now silent sky.

"COME BACK!" he roared, but no planes heeded his cry. When he saw it was futile, he turned his attention to the twins looking up at him from the foot of the tree. "Get back into the hole!" he ordered. "Get back into it right now! The war must come! The war will come!"

"It's over!" Dexter shouted.

"No!" the Secret Keeper wailed. "I will take you back down myself!"

He had a gun.

But when he aimed it the twins, the shifting of his weight caused a loud creaking among the branches. Then a crack.

"Oh, God," he said.

He tried to move through the treetop, but slipped and fell down through the branches, breaking them along the way. But he did not fall out. His robe caught and tangled, and he found himself hanging from the tree upside down out over the edge of Hellmouth.

The ash tree started to sway. Roots began to snap as it teetered on the brink.

"Damn you!" the Secret Keeper cursed, struggling with his robe. "Damn you, both!"

And then the great tree gave up its grip on the Earth and fell into the abyss.

The putrid smoke was gone, so the little group watched the tree fall until it was out of sight. When it hit bottom, the ground shook.

Earth began sliding into the hole.

The group hurried away. They could already hear sirens in the distance.

Dr. Fludd had her arm around Daphna. Dex had his around Nora.

Branwen and Wren were holding hands, as were Quinn's parents.

Not one of them looked back.

CHAPTER FIFTY-ONE
As Good a Story as Any

Daphna sat on a couch, looking through the giant photo album propped up on her lap.

Dex was sitting with Nora on another couch, watching his sister turn pages with happy tears in her eyes. "Dr. Fludd had them recovered from our house," he said, "*and* put them into new albums?"

Daphna nodded without looking up.

"And you told her to burn every single picture in Mr. G's house?"

Daphna nodded again.

No one else was in the waiting room. A TV mounted on the wall was showing one of those talking heads who seem to think shouting proves they know what they're talking about.

He was shouting that passing meteors were responsible for the weather anomaly, and that one of them crashed to Earth in Portland, Oregon, and that's all there was to this ridiculous nonsense. The crater had already collapsed in on itself, he ranted, but if it needed to be excavated to satisfy the loonies and conspiracy theorists, then he was all for it.

The whole angel bit with the Wax twins, he declared, was the government's Hollywood-style propaganda, special effects and all. Those kids were the perfect choices given their appearance in all the recent news! It was incredibly obvious that they were used to buy the President time to get to the bottom of it all! The government had no right to dupe its citizens and come next election, he was doomed!

The twins looked at each other when he finally finished raving. They shrugged. After speaking with the President themselves, they both thought he was a nice enough guy. He had a tough job.

"As good a story as any," Dex said.

Just then Doctor Fludd and Quinn's parents came out of Quinn's room. Dr. Brody came out behind them. He looked at Daphna and said, "Nurse Cates will be assigned to Quinn. She'll take good care of him. She's one of our best. I'm expecting a full recovery."

Dr. Fludd put her hand on Daphna's shoulder and smiled. "You can go in," she said. "He just woke up, and he asked for his angel."

CHAPTER FIFTY-TWO
The Business At Hand

Dex, Daphna, Quinn, and Nora sat in a circle on Mr. G's front porch. Across the street workers were just beginning to clear debris from what used to be Wilson High School.

In the center of their circle was a large cooler, on top of which sat a golden book with a key sticking out of its cover.

Daphna leaned forward and picked up the Holy Grail. "Are we sure we want to do this?" she asked.

Heads nodded nervously all around.

"I thought this would be a good place," Daphna said. "I guess—I don't know. I'm sorry for Mr. G—for *all* the Colors who gave up so much and searched so long, only to end up—I hope the Realm of Dead Souls is not the end of everything. But I guess we'll never know. I *hope* we'll never know."

No one spoke.

"We're agreed, right?" Daphna asked again.

Heads nodded again.

Daphna looked at the book in her perspiring hands. She ran her finger over the top edge of the key. Her heart was pounding. "I feel like I should rub the book first, to make a wish or something."

"Why don't you?" Quinn asked.

"I—" Daphna said, caught a bit off guard, "I don't even know what I'd—" But then she said, "Yes, I do. I know exactly what I'd wish for: I'd wish I didn't need to fit in so much, that I didn't feel so insecure about what popular people think of me. I thought I was over it, but I don't think I ever will be. Not completely, anyway. What would you wish for?"

"My parents are back," Quinn said, "and I'm with you. So I'd feel selfish to wish for anything. But still, I'd wish I could stop living so much in my head. I need to see the world a little more for what it actually is, especially now that I'm back in it."

Nora was sitting next to Quinn, so all eyes went to her. "I'd wish not to be so afraid of doing the wrong thing," she said. "Like I am right now. But I want to do this," she hastened to add. "I really do."

"I want to read," Dex said.

Daphna handed him the Grail.

Dex stared at the awesome object in hands, but after a moment he said, "I'm not going to ask for that, though. Or anything else." He handed the book back to his sister.

"But you deserve that wish, Dex," Daphna said. "You couldn't possibly deserve it more."

Dexter shrugged. "It's part of me," he said, "and it sounds like cutting out part of yourself—even if it's the part you don't like—maybe isn't the best idea in the world."

Daphna reached over and squeezed her brother's hand. Then she turned to the group and said, "Then we're ready? We're really going to do this?"

"I have a question," Nora said.

Everyone looked to her again.

"When Jesus took the book from Heaven, he must have known what it really was. He wanted to bring God to man. Why didn't he open it?"

The group considered the question for a moment, then Daphna, to no one's surprise, responded. "Maybe it's like we were thinking before," she speculated. "He didn't think the world was ready. Or, maybe he tried, but couldn't turn the key. If so, maybe he decided it wasn't for him to do and had the Templars hide it until they found someone who could. Maybe that's where all the sword in the stone stories came from. Maybe *that's* what the High Priests were actually trying to do every year in Holy of Holies. Maybe—"

"Daph," Dex said.

"Well," Daphna said, flushing. "She asked."

Nora smiled. "I guess we'll never know," she said.

"On that note," Daphna said, getting back to the business at hand. "Are we absolutely, one-hundred percent sure we're going to do this?"

"Yes," the others said.

"Okay. Let's do it."

Dex got up and opened the cooler.

Dry ice steam poured out.

When it wafted away, he lifted out Dr. Lewis' last

set of angel's wings. Quinn moved the cooler aside.

Daphna put the Holy Grail down on the porch, and Dex set the wings on it.

Everyone else stood up and, without consciously deciding to do so, linked hands.

For a moment, nothing happened, but then the wings began to twitch. A few moments later, they began to flutter. And then, with a single powerful flap, they heaved themselves into the air, taking the shining golden book with them.

The two couples rushed out onto the lawn, then into the street as it rose into the sky over the school.

The wings rose higher and higher until a jagged flash of light seemed to slice open the sky for just a moment.

After that moment, the Holy Grail was gone.

Dex and Daphna looked at each other and smiled. They'd both seen something in that flash. And they knew they'd both seen it.

Their mothers receiving the book.

All four kids stared into the empty sky now. And this time all four offered up wishes, wishes that might better be described as prayers. The words each chose were different, but they all meant the same thing:

May we now become the authors of our own lives.

ABOUT THE AUTHOR

David Michael Slater is an acclaimed author of books for children, teens, and adults. He teaches English to 8th graders, but you will not be required to write an essay after reading this book. David lives in Reno, Nevada with his wife and son. You can learn more about David and his work at www.davidmichaelslater.com.